THUNDER
STRUCK

BOOK 1 OF THE STORM CANYON SERIES

ANNA HAGUE

"In the steady gaze of the horse shines a silent eloquence that speaks of love, loyalty, strength, and courage. It is the window that reveals to us how willing is his spirit, how generous his heart."

L. McGuire

I visited South Dakota for the first time in 2019. I fell in love with the Black Hills area and especially Spearfish Canyon, and thus was the inspiration for Thunderstruck. This story is dedicated to my good friend Denise. Despite the heartache, being there for my special time meant the world to me. One day, we will get a trip for us that is perfect.

Thanks to all my author friends who always find time for me, my editor, who makes the story come alive and to Susan for finding all those silly little mistakes and giving her insight.

Cover by Nemo Designs
Edited by Delilah Devlin
Formatting by Glowing Moon Design and Formatting

INTRODUCTION

I hope you enjoyed Thunderstruck. This novella is the first story in the Storm Canyon Series. Rose, Lara, Dylan, and Keller will all get their own stories, and Maverick and Evangeline will continue their journey within those pages.

When I went to South Dakota in the summer of 2019 for the Wild Deadwood Reads book signing, my husband and I, along with two very good friends, made a vacation of it. I always wanted to go to Deadwood after watching the television series Deadwood. I'm a real history buff. What I wasn't prepared for was the vast beauty of the area. From the Badlands to the Black Hills, the scenery was incredible.

I knew because of that trip, a book would be

born. I know horse shifters are not real, but if they were, what a better place to be one than Spearfish Canyon.

South Dakota was breathtaking, awe inspiring, and even more than I envisioned. I cannot wait for the day I return.

CHAPTER ONE

Evangeline blinked several times to clear the blurriness from her eyes. The full moon cast a luminous radiance over the ranch even beyond the corrals—and the silver streak resembling a horse that raced across the grassy plain, bucking every few paces and whinnying at the obsidian night. She glanced at the half empty bottle of bourbon she clutched and back to the thundering steed glowing in the night.

"Oh hell, no." She'd been at the ranch for over three weeks and knew every horse in residence but had yet to see any running wild as spectacular as this one. The wild horses in the area were located at a sanctuary over an hour away in Hot Springs not in this part of the Black Hills.

"Damn, Jackson." She and the owner of the local

gas station, deli, laundry, and liquor store had been on a first-name basis since she perused the alcohol department as regularly as she could get to town. "What the hell did you sell me?" The bourbon didn't look or smell any different than anything else she'd purchased, but Jackson had suggested the Black Hills Recipe would be unlike any other bourbon she'd tried. Was it filtered through peyote or something? No, peyote wasn't native to South Dakota, but who really knew what went into locally distilled spirits?

"Ma'am."

Evangeline's heart stuttered at the masculine voice. "Keller, you startled me. What are doing out here in the dark?"

The cowboy whisked his hat from his head and raked his fingers through his dark blond hair. "I was just checkin' on the horses before I turned in. Up kind of late, aren't you?"

She swung her legs from the arm of the wooden rocker on the porch of her cabin. "I suppose. I don't have to get up early like you do, though."

"Still trying to find yourself out here?"

"Something like that."

Keller cocked his head to the bottle tucked in her fingers. "Was that full when you started the evening?"

She swirled the amber liquor. "Maybe."

"You be careful with any shit Jackson recommends." He stuffed his hat on head and tipped the brim to her. "Ma'am. Enjoy what's left of the evening while you can still remember."

He stepped away toward the bunkhouse. "Keller?"

"Yes, Ma'am?"

"Well, for one, would you stop calling me *ma'am?*"

He snickered. "Sorry, habit."

"Good manners." She set the bottle on the porch and rested her elbows on her knees. "Did you see a silver horse running across the meadow?"

"Tonight?"

"Like a few minutes ago."

"No, Ma...Miss Webber. I didn't."

"Evangeline. How about calling me Evangeline. I think I've been here long enough for that. Anyway, are you sure? It was bucking and whinnying and flying across the grass."

"I was in a barn full of horses. I hear lots of whinnying. Didn't see it, sorry."

Slumping back in the rocker, she sighed. Maybe she was hallucinating. The clearness she was seeking hadn't exactly presented itself since her arrival. The lure of the mountains and fresh air had brought her here. She needed a change, at least for a little while. The day to day survival wasn't working. She needed to snap out of her funk. It'd been two years. She needed to move on. That's what her friends and family said. She didn't see any of them having to handle what she did. Live with what she did.

"Well, must be the bourbon. Goodnight, Keller. I think I should hit the sack, too."

"Tomorrow's a new day," he said.

"That's what they say."

That's what they say.

WHATEVER HAD BEEN in the bourbon to cause her to hallucinate, the mystery ingredient did not give her a hangover like so many of her previous choices. Still, hallucinating should be enough to make a person stop drinking. Maybe tomorrow.

She lay still, listening to the morning songs of the Canyon Wren, Red-breasted Nuthatch, and Downy Woodpecker. She'd named her troubadours Sam, Pecan, and of course, Woody. Every morning, they were her alarm clock. Unfortunately, they ignored her requested nine a.m. wake-up call and promptly started in around six every morning.

"Morning, Sam, Pecan. Mornin' Woody." She stretched, threw off the quilt, and sat on the edge of the bed. "Do you guys ever sleep in?" Reaching for a hair band, she caught her dark chocolate brown hair in a ponytail before making her way to the bathroom.

The cabin came with a coffee maker and small refrigerator, but if she wanted hot food, she had to walk down the path past the barn and corrals to reach the ranch house where they served meals. She'd asked for the most isolated cabin, but since she'd arrived early in May, two snowstorms had made the walk not only cold, but a little treacherous. Today, however, the weather had turned more spring-like with a bright morning sun and a warm breeze rustling the pines.

She stepped from the cabin wearing hiking boots, Minnie Mouse leggings, an oversized sweatshirt, and carried her Mt. Rushmore coffee mug. She hadn't stayed at the ranch the entire time. She'd ventured out doing the tourist thing a few times, whenever she could bum a ride to town or tag along with a tourist group.

The tinkle of the brook running alongside of the path would give way to a wider stream flowing into the canyon. Evangeline had visited the waterfall that was a mile away numerous times, and today, she'd fill a backpack with water, snacks, and her camera, and then spend the day hiking before settling at the falls' edge to contemplate her distaste for planning any sort of a future.

Scents of bacon, pancakes, and coffee wafted through the air as she approached the ranch house. One end of the structure contained the offices, while the other housed a lounge area complete with an Old West-style bar and the dining hall shared by guests and ranch hands alike. Evangeline had found that most of the ranch's guests stayed no more than a week. By the time she made an attempt to get to know any of them, they were packing to go home. No matter. Her lengthy stay and physical proximity had her given her more of an opportunity to spend time with the workers and cowboys of the Silver Spear Canyon Ranch.

Even in the last three weeks, some of the cowboys she'd met when she'd first arrived had moved on and new ones replaced them. By nature, some cowboys seemed to be born under a wandering star and drifted, but never settled, any one place for long. Keller, she assumed, had been with the ranch for several years. The fortyish foreman was a native and had said on more than one occasion he'd die in the Black Hills and be laid to rest somewhere in Spearfish Canyon. Buck had to be at least sixty. The grizzled cowboy was a true drifter, who said he'd worked cattle and ranches all over the west. South Dakota winters didn't suit his arthritic bones, and he said he'd be moving on soon, but according to Keller, Buck had been saying the same thing for six years. He was full of tall tales for the guests, and he seemed to bask in the attention.

She'd found out Rose, Lara, and Dylan shared cooking, bartending and other guest duties. Rose and Lara used to live around Deadwood until they moved to the ranch, while Dylan had left Rapid City to find his calling as a beer slinging psychologist, cook and resident ladies' man.

"Mornin', Buck, Keller. How's it hanging?" She brushed passed the table filled with employees and headed for the serving line.

"About three feet," Buck mumbled and smiled into his tin coffee mug.

Evangeline let Rose pile bacon, potatoes, and pancakes on her plate. Way too much food, but what the hell? She was getting plenty of exercise, so what if she put on a few pounds? She was still down twenty. Nothing like trauma for a weight loss program—not that she'd recommended it.

Most of the guests didn't hit the early breakfast. They waited to a more city slicker decent hour. Evangeline preferred the first breakfast. Sitting alone when few were in the dining room was much less conspicuous than being solitary in a room full of chatty people. Kind of like being the kid with the peanut allergy in the school cafeteria.

She drowned her pancakes with syrup until the sweet liquid oozed over the short stack. She cut a section with her fork, scooped a piece of bacon and speared a chunk of potato, and stuffed the whole concoction into her mouth. Quite a breakthrough for someone who'd spent most of her life not allowing her food to touch. Something about this place had changed several things about her in the short time she'd stayed.

Then, there he was.

As she attempted to chew a too large bite, she saw him enter the room. Even if the room were full of gabby guests, they would have fallen silent at his arrival. He commanded attention even if he didn't ask for it. With biceps and thighs threatening to burst their confines of sleeves and jeans, the man reeked of the quintessential American cowboy in Wrangler jeans. Rick Cambios-Plata, aka the resident horse whisperer, kept a low profile around the ranch. He didn't interact much with the guests. Evangeline couldn't blame him there. Some had a lifetime ticket aboard the stupid train, and the few times she'd seen him on a trail ride with guests, he'd returned with an expression somewhere between God help him and murderous intent.

He filled a plate from the chafing dishes on the serving table and returned to the crammed-full employee table.

"Sorry, Mav." A few mumbled.

He glanced around the area and set his plate across from Evangeline. "May I join you, this morning?"

She swallowed the thick bite fearing it would lodge in her throat. Her gaze surveyed the room full of vacant tables. "Um, sure. Knock yourself out." Why on earth was he asking to sit with her?

He set his plate across from her and eased onto the wooden bench seat.

"You're a rather hearty eater, aren't you?" He drizzled a small amount of syrup over his tall stack without looking at her.

"Is that supposed to be a compliment?" Her fork clanged on the table when it fell from her grasp. Evangeline caught a hint of a smile from his down-turned face.

"I suppose." He rested his elbows on the table, and his fork was tucked between his thumb and forefinger. "A fair amount of the guests, namely the women, complain about the food. Not the taste, but the amount."

"Then I'd tell them just because it's there doesn't mean you have to eat it." She squirted more syrup on her pancakes and resumed assembling her breakfast combo. "It's been a long time since I could enjoy food. I'm sure I've gained weight. At this point in life, I'm not trying to impress anyone anymore, so fuck it. I'm eatin' it. Screw it, I mean. Sorry. I have trouble with what comes out of my mouth."

His eyes were the color of dark cocoa, and his mirthful gaze seemed to penetrate clear through to view the contents of her stomach. "Me, too. That's why I try to stay away from the guests."

"*Okaayy*, then why are you sitting here with me?" Her coffee was no longer warm, but she wasn't about to get up to retrieve more. He hadn't spoken more than a few words to her since she'd arrived. She was fascinated by him, and who was she kidding? She'd like nothing more than to impress him.

"Miss Webber, you've been here so long, I'm beginning to think of you as one of the employees. I've seen you sweeping the porch, tending the campfire, helping Keller feed the horses, sometimes. You're paying the Silvers to work here."

He had a point, but there was only so much hiking and riding a person could do day after day after day. She loved the sounds of the ranch, the canyon, and rushing streams, along with the peace nature gave her, but inactivity was hard for her.

Doing little things around the ranch had given her a sense of belonging.

At least for now, she couldn't go back to the life she'd known. So what if people said she was hiding, afraid to move on. They weren't completely wrong. She just didn't know where to move on to.

"It's only little things. Doesn't amount to much." She debated leaving a few bites on her plate but didn't contemplate long before scraping the plate clean of any crumbs. "Can, I ask you a question?"

"Sure, as long as it doesn't involve politics, religion, world affairs, Hollywood, millennials, soccer, or foodies."

She cocked her with amusement. "I think I'm safe. I heard some of the guys call you 'Mav.' I thought your name was Rick." Her eyebrow raised in question. She supposed people went by more than one name. People referred to her as Angi, Lina, and a few other names she'd rather not answer to.

"Maverick. My full first name is Maverick." He pushed his plate aside, leaving way more food on the plate than she had.

"So, you're a horse guy named Maverick. Interesting."

"More than you know."

He started to rise and gathered his plate, utensils and mug. "Miss Webber, have a good day."

"Wait, one more question." She tapped her thumb on the table questioning whether she should ask. "Did you happen to see a greyish silver horse running around last night…late?"

A voice from the other table boomed, "You saw the Ghost Horse?"

CHAPTER TWO

Evangeline's head whipped to the freckled-faced, young ranch hand. "Ghost horse?" Maverick rolled his eyes. "Drink much Miss Webber?" He carried his plate to the bus bin and left the dining hall.

Keller pushed away from the table and stood. "What she saw came out of bottle of a Jackson Garrity recommendation." The other men roared with laughter. He turned to young man. "Polk, it's all a bunch of nonsense. There's no ghost horse runnin' about Spearfish Canyon. You want ghost stories, go into Deadwood. Whole town's full of 'em.

"Come on, boys. Got fifteen horses to saddle up." Keller's boots scraped on the planked floor as he carried his plate to the plastic bin set out for dirty dishes.

A shuffling of chairs and mingling of voices erupted as the group emptied the table and proceeded out the door. Evangeline's ear warmed from a nearby breath. His voice startled her as she was still thinking about Rick's departure.

"Stop listenin' to Jackson, or we're gonna find you face down in Spearfish Creek, and that's bad for business."

She cocked her head away from Keller's voice, and her gazed traveled to face. He winked. "Why? What's in it? Peyote?"

"Ha ha. Who knows?" Keller left her to ponder if she'd really been hallucinating last night.

INSTEAD OF HIKING one of the many trails around the ranch, Evangeline chose to follow the creek for a few hours, only stopping to rest to cool her toes in the frigid water or acquiesce to other visitors' requests for her to take their photos. She'd dabbled in photography over the years and always found the best angle and backdrop for people to remember their trip when they thumbed through photos. While much of the creek ran along the side of the road, the sound of invading cars was minimal. The barrage of tourists wouldn't come until later in the summer she'd been told, but South Dakota winters had no problem extending into May.

Today, however, proved to be much warmer than she'd anticipated, and by noon, she'd shed two of her three layers and now sat atop a boulder sipping water and eating an apple. The rest of her lunch, packed by the staff, she'd eat on her way back. Dinner wasn't until seven in the evening. She needed to go to town again to stock up on snacks, but she had to take advantage of the hospitality of ranch guests or the staff to get there. Strange not having a car, but oddly freeing.

A rustling and voices in the trees not far from the creek's bank snared her attention.

"You got a signal yet?"

"No."

"Dammit, we're going to die out here, all because you thought you were fucking Lewis and Clark."

Evangeline chuckled. How silly they'd feel in about a minute when they emerged and saw the road above the embankment.

"Look. There's a woman. Thank God. Can you help us?" A woman, maybe in her late twenties, and a man of similar age teetered across the rocks in the creek to her boulder.

"Are you lost?" Evangeline asked. Of course, they

were. She found toying with people could be enormous fun.

They were dressed in all the appropriate gear of people who'd gone to an outdoor store and let the salesperson talk them into five hundred dollars of "must haves" for the wilderness. They had everything they needed for hiking Mt. Kilimanjaro. A little overkill for the Black Hills when they were without any snow.

"Yes, of course we're lost. Can you help us?" The woman shrugged out of her backpack and dug inside until she produced a canteen.

"Do you need directions?"

The man sighed. "Could you call someone to come get us and take us back to the lodge? My phone doesn't have a signal."

"Which lodge is that?" Evangeline stayed on the boulder as she asked her questions. They looked harmless, inept really, but you never knew.

"The Mirran Lodge," the woman said, after tipping the canteen all the way and swallowing what must have been the last few drops.

Mirran Lodge was a few miles away from the ranch. A long few miles, if they were already this far. "Sorry, I don't have a phone. You could either follow the creek or follow the road, and you'll eventually find the sign for the lodge."

"How far is that?" The man took the canteen from the woman, lifted it to his lips, but frowned. "Thanks for drinking all the water."

Seriously, they got all the way out here and only brought one canteen of water? "Staying on the road, you're looking at about seven or eight miles."

"Are you fuckin' kidding me?" The woman's screeching caused an osprey to take flight from its nest. Damn, she had a range.

She turned to the man and began poking her finger into his chest. "I'm not walking eight miles. I'm not walking anymore. I didn't want to come out here in the first place with the bears, mountain lions, and God knows what else. You walk your ass to the lodge, get our car, and come pick me up. I'll wait with her."

Oh hell, no.

"Fine."

"Lewis" began the steep climb up the embankment toward the road, while "Clark" huffed and rested against my boulder. The osprey returned, announcing her arrival with a loud squawk, and Clark whipped around so fast, she almost laid herself out in the water. "What was that?"

"Probably a bear," Evangeline drawled.

Clark grabbed the backpack, and water flew all around as she splashed through the creek, forgetting about using the rocks as a bridge "Damian, wait. Wait up!"

Black bears were not common visitors to the area. A miniscule twinge of guilt fluttered briefly through her. Maybe she hadn't been very nice, but she had her peace and quiet back. She reached into her small pack and pulled out her phone. She pressed the one contact she still talked to.

"Hey, Lily. Whatcha doin'?" She called her sister once a week, but had refused to give her much insight regarding her future.

"Angi, I know I ask you this every week, but when are you coming home?" Lily gave a dramatic sigh. Evangeline could see her younger sister's face—Shakespeare tragedy at its best.

Evangeline shrugged although her sister couldn't see it. "I don't know. It's easier here."

"It's been two years."

"Yes, I know. I went through the motions for two years, and I couldn't do it anymore. I'm tired of people telling me to get over it, move on, you've got a life to live. And quite honestly, I didn't think I'd be hearing it from you, too."

"Angi, I'm doing it for selfish reasons. I miss my sister, and I'm getting married, and I want you here for that. I need you here for that."

"Married? When did this happen?" Lily was

dating a guy, and had been for a few years, but marriage had never come up.

"Dan proposed on Saturday, finally."

"Did you give him some sort of ultimatum?" A breeze began moving through the canyon, and Evangeline began to chill. She wanted to end the call so she could put her jacket on. She wanted the call to end to cut the connection to her outside world.

"Didn't have to. Jacob Meyer moved into the apartment next to me." Lily's high school sweetheart. She knew Lily had no intention of getting back with Jacob, but clearly Dan believed she might.

"As long as it's not in the next month, I'll make it to the wedding. Look, I gotta go. My phone is dying. Love you."

"Love you too. I miss…"

She ended the call before Lily could finish. She loved her sister and missed her, but unless her sister hopped a plane and joined her, Evangeline wouldn't be seeing her until the wedding. Here in Spearfish and far from Santa Barbara, the memories didn't possess her mind as easily as they did back home. Home. She called the area her home, but home was where you were supposed to be happy and comfortable, and Evangeline hadn't been either. So, she'd left.

Spearfish Canyon in the Black Hills region was

so far removed from what she'd known. Life was simpler without people knowing what had happened. Then, there was the horses. She'd grown up around horses, loved everything about them— their feel, their scent, their obliviousness of being the most magnificent creature God had ever created. Grown up life had taken her away from horses—but here, she could revel in their gloriousness without judgement. An old cowboy who had worked for the family where she'd kept her horse as a teenager had once told her, "They're nothing so wrong with the inside of a man, the outside of a horse can't cure." She smiled at his wisdom. Although, the quote actually belonged to Winston Churchill, and the cowboy had revised it to suit himself, but still, he was right. Being at the ranch around the horses had eased some of her pain.

A long drawn-out sigh escaped her mouth. She'd better begin her journey back to the ranch. She didn't want to leave her spot, but the six miles back would take time, and she didn't want to be out in the woods once the sun began setting. Also, the thought of being late for dinner wasn't pleasant. Rick, or Maverick, was right. She was a hearty eater. Good thing she was past the point in life where impressing someone wasn't a priority.

CHAPTER THREE

Dinner was different from breakfast. They only served once, which meant all the guests were in the dining room at the same time. For that reason, the cowboys were absent. The kitchen sent their dinner down to the bunkhouse. Evangeline enjoyed listening to the good-hearted banter between the ranch hands, but instead, tonight, she sat at one of the long tables with a family from—she couldn't believe her bad luck—from the Santa Barbara area. The parents were fortyish, a few years older than her. They had two boys and a girl, twelve, nine, and the girl was seven. The children, Kyle, Grady, and Pressly, were home-schooled so that's why the family could up and take off anytime. Evangeline knew all of this because Mom had proceeded to tell her all of their background. When she found out where Evangeline was from, she'd been somehow elevated to vacation best friend status. What were the odds?

Keller strode through the door, coffee mug in hand. As he was pouring coffee from the pot on the warmer, his gaze connected with Evangeline's.

"You." He made a beeline to her table.

Evangeline thumped her hand on her chest. "Me? What…what'd I do."

Coffee slopped over the side of the mug when he slapped it on the table. "I was coming from town today and saw this couple alongside the road waving all frantic. So, I stopped, and they jumped in my truck. Woman's all hysterical about bears and being lost. When she finally stopped shrieking, I was able to get out of her that they were lost, and they'd managed to find someone, and that someone told them there were bears all around, and they were lucky to be alive. When they described her, sounded an awful lot like you."

Evangeline chewed her lip. "It may have been me…but I didn't say there were bears everywhere."

"Then where did she get the notion?" Keller's green eyes flashed with accusations.

"She heard a sound and was all 'what was that?', and I may have said 'it could be a bear.'" Evangeline sat straighter. "I didn't say it was. I've never seen a bear around here. It was an Osprey flapping around. Not my fault they're dumbasses."

Keller straightened as well. He crossed his arms across his chest. "Had to spend the whole time listenin' to both of them going on about their ordeal. Longest seven miles of my life."

She couldn't repress the grin spreading from ear to ear. "I'd say I'm sorry, but that'd be a lie. Got 'em out of my hair. Besides, who doesn't love a cowboy savin' the day."

He growled and fled toward the door.

Evangeline's new best friend folded her napkin and placed the cloth across her empty plate. "You're a guest here, aren't you?"

Evangeline nodded. "Uh huh."

"Doesn't seem like a very nice way to treat a guest."

Soaking up the last of the mashed potatoes and gravy on her roll, Evangeline said, "Well, I've been here so long, we kinda have a comfortable relationship going."

"Ohhh."

Evangeline shook her head and popped the final bite into her mouth. Time for dessert. "Not that kind of relationship. Just friendly. I've been helping out a little here."

"How long are you staying?"

How long was she staying? Until she got her shit together.

"Probably a while. I like it here. If you'll excuse me, I think I'll take my pie to my room to eat later." She pushed away from the table and stood before cramming a spoon in her back jean pocket and picking up the plate filled with a slice of cherry pie.

Like most nights in the canyon, the ebony sky sparkled with thousands of stars. She'd never realized how few stars a person saw when living in highly populated areas. There was never complete darkness anywhere. Even when she went to the ocean at night, the beach was always backlit from homes, headlights, or streetlights. If the ranch turned off all the lights, a complete blanket of black would cover them all. As she made her way to her cabin, she noticed light coming through the trees. She followed the path that led to the corral separate from the area where the rest of the horses were kept. As she stepped from the wooded path into the clearing, she saw in the lit corral an undernourished and sway-backed horse standing in the center. Rick stood inside, leaning against the rails while watching the timid animal. He turned at her approach but said nothing and, instead, returned to watching the horse.

"What are you doing?" she asked, resting her

arms across the top rail, still holding the plate with her slice of pie.

"We're getting to know each other."

"He or she looks awful. What happened?"

Rick never took his eyes from the horse. "She. Found her at an auction. She'd have went to the killers."

"Killers?"

Even in the dim light, Evangeline could see anger in his dark eyes. "They buy horses for slaughter."

"Isn't that illegal?"

"Domestic slaughtering, yes. Horses are sent to Mexico or Canada where it's legal. Lots of countries consume horsemeat. I, uh, it's not something I like to think about."

"I didn't realize. That makes me sad...and angry." She moved the hand holding the pie closer to Rick. "Want pie?"

"Nah, thank you, though."

She bent, set the plate on the ground, and then climbed onto the fence. Throwing one leg over the top rail, she straddled the metal fence. "How long has she been here?"

"Couple weeks." Rick shoved off from the fence and stepped one pace toward the mare. She snorted and backed away from his advance. "We're making progress. She's not quite ready to trust though."

"Progress? Doesn't look like she wants anything to do with you." Evangeline loved horses and had spent a great deal of her youth riding. Never had she'd seen fear in horses' eyes like she saw in this one's. What had happened to her?

"This is the first time she's stood still for any amount of time with me in the corral. Normally, she's stomping and running back and forth across the corral." He rubbed his hand through his hair and retreated to the fence. "We're practically best friends now."

She swung her other leg across the rail and hooked both feet around the lower bar. At one time, the horse had been beautiful. Her ragged coat would have shone with a brilliant chestnut, Evangeline imagined. Her stomach began to turn with the anger churning inside. She hated her own kind. People were so cruel to creatures who had no recourse. A tear began to trickle down her cheek. "It's so unfair."

Rick cut her a skidways glance. "Humans are capable of great love and great cruelty. And both are acceptable. People may say it's wrong and bristle, but that's about as far as things go. Ire only goes as far as it's comfortable. Little ever changes."

"What will or can you do for her?"

The mare seemed to calm a bit and began skimming the ground with her nose, snuffling as she searched for a tidbit of food.

"If I can get her to trust again, and feel she'll be comfortable being around people, we might use her for a trail horse. Guide horse, I mean. If not, I'll find a place where she can be safe, have plenty to eat, and be happy."

"Where's that?" She knew about the wild horse sanctuary in ……….but didn't think a domesticated one would work there.

"I have a place I use."

Evangeline waited, but Rick didn't elaborate. None of her business she figured. "Am I bothering you?"

"Not really."

She wasn't sure how to take his answer. Did he mean she wasn't bothering him, or was she, and he was polite enough to say so? Unwrapping her legs from the rails, Evangeline slipped to the ground on the other side of the fence. "I'll leave you two to, uh, do whatever you were doing. Goodnight."

"Ms. Webber." He pointed to the ground. "Don't forget your pie." His hat and the night shadowed his face, but she could tell he was smiling.

Relief coursed through her. Maybe she wasn't bothering him. "Thanks. Maybe I'll see you in the morning when I'm scarfing down my *hearty* breakfast."

"After you do, you might need some exercise. Want to go for a ride?"

Ride. She hadn't noticed him leading any of the trail rides. "Are you the guide tomorrow?"

He laughed. "Hell no, only as a last resort. I mean a ride on a different trail. Not one we use for the guests, but I want to see if it might be viable for future use. Weather can wreak havoc on the trails. I can tell you're pretty experienced. The other rides must seem pretty boring for you."

She wasn't sure if she liked the thought he'd been watching her, or was he being creepy? If a stalker was hot, was he still a stalker? "I would love a different ride. It's not like I don't like the regular trail, but you're right, after a while, it's a...well, the scenery doesn't change much."

Without looking at her, he said, "Well then, I'll see you after breakfast. Dress warmer; we're going higher."

CHAPTER FOUR

The horses climbed for nearly an hour—not a steep haul, but a steady and low-grade rise. To her surprise, Rick had saddled Baxter for her. Baxter was a cowboy horse used for leading the trail rides. He was not a nose-to-tail horse like many trail horses, and often displayed his displeasure at having to maintain a slower gait. He was spirited, for sure, and Evangeline had drooled over the beautiful bay since she'd arrived.

With every step, she reveled in the powerful horse's spirit. For the first twenty minutes, he tested her, dancing around until Rick and his mount moved away from the barn and onto the trail. Baxter wanted to take the lead, but she relegated him to second. He snorted. She laughed and hoped at some point the trail gave way to open space. She'd love to let him have his head and feel the rhythmic glide of powerful hooves sailing across the ground.

"Does this ever level out?" She squeezed Baxter's sides and moved him alongside Rick, who'd said virtually nothing since they'd left the ranch.

"Not on the way up, but on the way back we pass through two canyons with plenty of level ground."

"Level enough to let loose? I bet Baxter would love a good length to stretch his legs."

Rick adjusted his dusty black Resistol hat. Evangeline noticed lines of scars across his olive-skinned hand. The corners of his mouth upturned in an ever so slight smile. "I don't believe there's a big enough piece of land to give him all the stretchin' he wants. Damn horse's got to be part Arabian. He's got an attitude and can run forever. Hot blood for sure."

"We're gettin' along okay."

"He respects you. Figured out pretty fast you wouldn't take any shit from him."

Pine, damp earth, and the sweet scent of mountain air and wildflowers invaded her nose. No car exhaust up here. The ride up along the narrow trail and, at times, rocky path had been more challenging than the one she and the guests used. Maybe not for beginners, but those who had ridden horses would love the twisty trail and stunning views. "So, do you think you'll use this trail? It's a great ride. I mean, a sunset ride would be glorious."

He pulled his dun mare to a halt. "You're right about a sunset ride. And maybe guests could do it, but there's some tricky parts to maneuver."

Evangeline examined the ground they'd covered. "Maybe use it for experienced riders, only. I remember the waiver paperwork asking for level of experience."

Rick chuckled. "You know how many people check the "expert" box, and fifteen minutes into the ride, fall off their horse?"

"A lot?"

"Too many to count. Although, some of the cowboys may instigate more testing of skills than they should. Can't say I blame 'em. They get bored." He reached around to the bag attached to the end of the saddle and pulled out two water bottles. "Here."

Evangeline was grateful for the water. Normally, when she left the ranch, no matter where she was going, she packed water and snacks. This morning, she may have had some nerves about riding with Rick. "Thanks."

She unscrewed the cap and swallowed several drinks of the ice cold water. Even though the temps were cool this high up, she'd still worked up a thirst handling Baxter. "Don't suppose you brought any snacks in that bag?"

He side-eyed her.

"I forgot to bring any and, seeing as how I'm a hearty eater, I'm a little hungry."

"Sorry, but if you're that desperate, we could forage on the ground for something."

She gulped the remaining water before crushing the pliable plastic and handing it back to Rick. He stuffed the two empty bottles in the bag, turned his mount and around, and said. "Let's head back before you disintegrate."

Evangeline huffed. "I'm fine. I don't want to go back."

He winked. "This is halfway. We're headin' back anyway."

Baxter began to side step. She wrangled him under control and urged him forward next to Rick. "You know, you're not very nice, sometimes."

"Never claimed or aimed to be."

The trek down wound through groves of Ponderosa Pines, Birch, and Box Elders. Rick was quiet, but she was enjoying the sounds of the wood-peckers, an occasional eagle, and the wispy breeze ruffling her hair. She missed nothing from her home in California. Maybe, the memories were too much, but bumping along on the narrow trail was about as peaceful as life could be.

As the breeze increased, she thought she heard something other than birds. She gave a slight tug on the reins, signaling Baxter to stop. "Did you hear that?" she asked Rick.

He stopped and twisted in the saddle. "Hear what?"

She scanned the trees and boulders but didn't see or hear anything else. "I thought I heard a horse neighing. Are we close to the other trail?"

"Mmm, nope."

"Any wild horses up here?" She continued to scrutinize her surroundings.

"No. Horses don't usually hang out in the woods. They kinda prefer open areas." He turned and clucked for his horse to move again. "If you want to get to flat ground to run Baxter, then we'd better get movin'."

"I swear I heard a horse."

CHAPTER FIVE

As soon as Evangeline dismounted, she knew the ride had been much more vigorous than the other rides. Her knees almost buckled, and her thighs begged for mercy. She hadn't realized how much she'd hugged Baxter's belly with her legs. A glass of wine and stint in the hot tub should help. After lunch.

Wait, she glanced at her watch. The face said one-thirty. She'd missed lunch. Maybe the staff would let her make a sandwich. Even if she had a car here, she was too sore to drive to town.

Keller stepped in to loosen the girth on Baxter's saddle. "They saved you a plate."

She handed Keller the reins and smiled. "Is my appetite that well known?"

He began to lead the horse away. "Darlin', you haven't missed a meal since you've been here."

She slipped two fingers in the waistband of her jeans. Maybe she did need to cut back a little, but not today. With slow and measured steps, Evangeline made her way up the path to the dining hall where someone had stashed a bowl of chili, a grilled cheese sandwich, and crackers into a warming oven.

Her mouth watered at the heaping bowl of goodness and gooey heaven that awaited. She gathered the meal and sat at the table closest to the kitchen. Lara was on her heels with a glass of iced tea.

"So, did you enjoy your ride with Mav?" Her Cheshire-cat grin loomed in Evangeline's face.

"The *ride* was fine." She wasn't sure the heat in her cheeks was from the first bite of the spicy chili or spending the last several hours with Rick.

"So, what happened?" She leaned across the table as if waiting for Evangeline to spill some long hidden secret.

Crumbling a handful of saltines into the bowl and stirring until they were mush, Evangeline considered her time up on the beautiful trail. Other than another off-handed insult and some complements about her riding ability, nothing noteworthy, swoon worthy, or worthy period had happened between them. "It's a fabulous trail. I'm sure people would love the views, if they're good enough riders. At times, the trail can be a little challenging. I had a great time."

Lara stiffened. "That's it?"

"Pretty much."

She narrowed her eyes at Evangeline. "So, he didn't say anything? Like he wanted to do something else—show you something?"

Evangeline hated cryptic. "No, just spit it out. What are getting at?"

Lara blew a breath and rested her chin in her cupped hand. "Maverick likes you. That's a big deal. He never hangs around the guests. We've all been talking about it."

A shiver began in her toes and shimmied all the way up her spine. Her flushed face was not from the chili. "Okay, this is not high school. I'm thirty-five years old. I don't need a band of teenagers passing notes back and forth determining if Rick is going to ask me out. Nothing he's said or done indicates attraction to me, and the same goes for me, too."

"Oh, please." She snorted. "Every time he's anywhere near, your eyes are glued to him. Plus, he does the same thing. And you're both about the same age. You're destined for each other."

A large chunk of grilled cheese pushed settled in her throat, forcing her to cough and reach for the tea. After she drank half, Evangeline slapped the glass on the table. She held up a finger. "One, I'm from California. The commute would be a bitch, and two, I'm not looking for a relationship."

"When you're not looking is the best time. Hell, you might as well stay here; you been here over a month already." She patted the table as she stood. "Mark my words, you and Maverick have a very special connection, and you'll see it."

Lara left her to finish the food that now didn't seem quite as palatable as it had a few minutes ago. There was no denying Rick had everything going for him, physically, to make her think about what being with a man again might be like. He was nice enough in his own way, but she wasn't ready. No, she wasn't sure if she'd ever be ready. She would just keep enjoying the ranch and the pleasant banter between her and Rick.

Keep telling yourself that.

She set the empty dishes in the bus pan on the cart near the exit of the dining hall. The glass of wine and hot tub couldn't come soon enough.

THE SUN'S rays warmed her face. Evangeline rested her head against the concrete edge of the hot tub.

She'd immersed herself up to her neck in soothing bubbles. A glass of wine sat empty nearby, and she considered raising her arm in the chilly afternoon to pour another. She closed her eyes to meditate—free her mind of anything and everything, but images of Rick kept trolling her brain. It's not like they were bad images. No, not at all. Any image of the aloof cowboy had its good points. A naked image might even have better points.

Evangeline opened her eyes to discern how big the cloud was that had moved across her sunshine. It wasn't a cloud at all, but her imagination come to life.

"Shit." She sat up and whirled her body to face Rick standing above her, scuffed cowboy boots and all.

"Did I disturb you?"

"Your knack for the obvious is amazing." She hoped no drool had been running down her chin. Not from sleeping, but her visualization of Rick in the flesh paralleled fresh-baked brownies. "I may have been dozing, a little. The water is massaging some muscles that got a little more workout than usual this morning."

He grinned. "You like working out those muscles?"

She poured herself another glass of liquid

courage. "Not a fan of organized exercise, although I don't mind getting the heart beating a little faster now and then." Taking a big swig and checking her breasts to see no one had slipped out of the swimsuit, she said. "Was there something you wanted?"

He crouched, giving her a view of how snug his jeans were in certain areas. "You said earlier that the trail rides were fine, but the scenery didn't change. You interested in a change of scenery?"

A twinge in her thigh reminded her why she was in the tub. "I'm not sure I could do another four hours in the saddle today."

"Didn't really mean that kind of scenery. You never leave the ranch much, so I was wondering if you'd be interested in goin' and gettin' some dinner and a little whiskey that won't make you... hallucinate?"

Lara's words rang in her head but scared her. When she hadn't thought Rick had any interest in her, fantasizing had been easy and fun. If by offering dinner, he really did have an interest in her, then the thought terrified her. She wasn't ready. She'd never be ready—not so much ready but the possibility of destroying someone else's life—well, she couldn't live through that again. Then again, she would go back to California...sometime, and so starting a relationship would be stupid, and so what would be wrong with a little dinner and…?

"Hello?" Rick's voice stopped the monologue in her head. "If it takes that much consideration then maybe it wasn't a good idea." He stood, stuffed his hat back on his head and walked away.

"No, no, wait." She called after him. "That's not it. I was, um, just thinking if I had something on my calendar I'd forgotten about."

He raised an eyebrow. "Calendar? Out here? You have a calendar?"

"Not so much a calendar, but you know sometimes people ask you if you want to do something later, and you say yes but you're not really sure. You know, that kind of thing." She downed the wine. Surely, she'd make more sense drunk than she was sober.

"I see. Well, when you get dried off and check your *calendar*, let me know. I wouldn't want to cause any conflicts." He turned again to leave.

"Wait, again." She really sucked at flirtation and anything else related to dating. When only one man had ever taken her on a date, then the skills were rusty, or maybe nonexistent. "I would like to go with you. I don't have a calendar. I just…can I just leave it at that before I make things worse?"

He chuckled. "Evangeline Webber, I'm not sure

you could make it any worse. We can go after all the horses are taken care of. Probably around six, six thirty."

"Okay, I'll be ready in my finest." *Oh my fucking God. I didn't just say that.*

"We don't have a country club around here," he said.

"I only brought jeans."

CHAPTER SIX

Evangeline wasn't sure the Canyon Saloon was designed to be an Old West dive, or was really one of those off-the-map dives serving the best food no one knew about. The aroma of grilled steaks, onions, whiskey, and freshly baked bread made her stomach growl. Loud enough for Rick to hear.

"I'd say to get a drink first, but sounds like you're in dire need of food."

"No, no. it's fine. I'd like a drink first."

Rick raised two fingers, catching the bartender's eye. The woman behind the bar acknowledged his request.

"So, you come here often?" Evangeline scanned the roughhewn shiplap walls adorned with neon beer signs and black and white photos of old cowboys and Native Americans, and a few Frederic Remington and Charles Russell prints.

Any other time, she'd have plenty of witty things to say, but what just came out of her mouth was one of the lamest things she'd ever said. Then again, when was the last time she'd been on a date…high school?

"If you mean, when I take an occasional day off, then yes, I usually come here."

A server sat two glasses of whiskey in front of them. Evangeline picked up the glass, sniffed, and swirled the amber liquid. "Smells awesome. What is it?"

Rick raised his glass. "Badlands Distillery. Best around."

She mirrored his toast and tasted the whiskey. The drink warmed her tongue and throat as she swallowed. This was miles above what she'd been drinking the night she saw the horse. Maybe she had been hallucinating. "This is really good. Thank you for bringing me here. I'm excited about the food, too."

"Of course you are." The smile creeping across his made her blush.

Upon closer inspection, Evangeline noticed his brown eyes were deep, deep brown, like the dark chocolate she loved to savor and let melt in her mouth. "You know, I haven't been on a da...I mean, out to dinner in a while."

"I haven't been on too many *dates*. Either too busy, or I don't find too many people that interesting."

"So, where do I fall on that scale?"

"Both."

"Is there a percentage?" She took another drink. "Never mind. I don't want to know." She tipped the glass and emptied the contents. "May I have another?"

She smiled at Rick's amused expression.

"Sure." He emptied his own glass and motioned for two more. "What I do know about you, I find interesting. However, other than your ability to ride and your affinity for alcohol and food, I don't know much about you except for your name address and credit card on file."

As the server set two more whiskey's in front of them, Evangeline cocked her head and narrowed her gaze at her way too attractive companion. "Credit card? Why would you have access to my credit card?"

"I have access to everything. It's part of being a family business."

"Family business? I didn't realize. Family, as in how and how many?"

"Jim and Betty are my parents."

"But wait. Their name is Silver, and your name... well, hell, I should have figured out Plata." She shook head in disgust.

"You bilingual or something?"

"My work. *When I work*, I'm a translator. So why the change?"

He leaned back as the server set down a plate with a cowboy ribeye and baked potato oozing melted butter and sour cream. Evangeline did the same, but her sizzling choice was sirloin and mashed potatoes.

"When my parents wanted to start the ranch, they figured Silver would be easier business-wise, and Silver Spear Ranch had a better sound than Cambios-Plata. I was adopted, and when I was old enough to make a choice, I chose to go with the real name."

"When were you adopted?"

"I was just a baby. Keller and me are the same age, so we've always been brothers."

"I think it's good to stay with your heritage. I'll probably go back to my maiden name soon." Evangeline hadn't told anyone she'd been married. Two Badlands whiskeys in, she wasn't seeing things, but she was on the verge of spilling her life.

"So, you were married?" The steak sat untouched, but Rick sipped his drink.

"My husband died. No. Well, I mean, he did. It's just complicated." A familiar and unwelcome flush invaded her body. She stopped talking and cut into her steak.

"So, what is your maiden name?"

She brushed a strand of dark hair from her face that had escaped the messy bun. "Cortés."

Rick's glass began to slip from his hand, but he caught hold and set the glass down hard on the table. He swallowed. "So, your family dates back to Spain. Was it an easy career choice, translating?"

"Not Spain, Mexico, actually. I'm second generation Mexican-American, and not as easy as you might think. My grandparents, when they moved to California from Mexico, they wanted to assimilate and wouldn't allow their kids to speak Spanish. So, my dad couldn't speak Spanish. When I was born, they regretted their decision and made sure both me and my sister could speak it. When the two of us were with them, we only spoke Spanish. We'd go home and try speaking to my dad. He didn't understand, and mom was originally from Indiana before her family moved to California, so she never learned. Wasn't always easy. Now, it's cool to know other languages. I do French and Italian, too, but mostly Spanish, and Spanish from Spain, *as well*. It's a little different."

Lost in her explanation, Evangeline didn't notice Rick's fidgeting with food until she inhaled and took a sip of the water their server had set on the table. "Is something wrong? You seem distracted...or bored, maybe."

Rick slung back the rest of his whiskey. "Oh, no, no. Not at all. I, uh. I was just pondering the name. *Cortés*. Related to the explorer?"

She laughed and shrugged. She may live among the pretty people and some of them famous, but she had no blue blood in her heritage. "Ha. I seriously doubt that. We're about as nondescript as they come."

RUBBING his hand along his jawline, Rick mused. "Hmmm.Cortés."

CHAPTER SEVEN

"**D**ammit, Keller, fuckin' wake up." Maverick pounded on the door of his brother's cabin but turned the knob and let himself inside.

"Keller!" he called through the darkness.

A yawning Keller, dressed only in boxers, shuffled into the room as an overheard light switched on. "What the fuck? Date not go well? Maybe if you'd go out more often, you'd still be in practice."

"Her name is Cortés. Her maiden name is Cortés."

Keller snickered and rubbed a hand through a thatch of bed head hair. "I guess that explains why you get a woody every time she walks by."

"I wasn't expecting this." Maverick stomped to the fridge and yanked a bottle of beer from the shelf. He twisted the cap, and the stainless steel sink twanged when he toss it inside. He downed half the bottle in one drink before resting his hands, still holding the bottle against the counter.

"Feel better?" Keller's wry grin did not help.

"No."

Keller went to the crackled brown leather loveseat and snatched a T-shirt. He pulled the shirt over his head and flopped sank into a cushion. "Look, this a good thing. She's royalty. You lucky bastard." He stifled another yawn. "Being a Cortés sure explains a lot. Has she said anything about...?

A bubble, and then a loud belch, moved from Maverick's throat and out of his mouth, which didn't taste near as good coming out as when the food and drink had gone down. "I'm not sure she knows. It's there. I can sense it, but she said her mother is originally from Indiana, and there's no clusters or sanctums east of the Mississippi. It's really the other part that worries me."

"You mean, why she's here?"

"Yeah. She's been her for weeks. Her reservation is open-ended. Is it really because she just needed to get away and recharge?" He started to tip the beer again, thought better of it, and sat the bottle in the sink. The belch was the tip of the iceberg. The hoppy liquid hadn't settled well in his stomach. He knew better than to eat the steak, but damn if it hadn't tasted good. "I think she's hiding something, but I'm not sure if it has anything to do with the ranch."

"My advice…" Keller rested his head against the top of the sofa and closed his eyes. "Find out, but don't blast your way in as you usually do. Ease into her. She's hotter than hell. Slow burn. Slow burn. Now, get the hell out. I drew the sunrise ride. I need some sleep."

"How did you draw sunrise. Did you forget you're the boss?" Maverick walked to the door, his body less rigid than when he'd arrived.

"Lane and Carew are down with some bug, and well, this particular group is some corporate bunch of assholes on some teambuilding bullshit. They're spendin' a shit ton of money, and I'd rather not send Buck out doing two hours of the Wild Bill Hickok in Deadwood show, when what comes out of his mouth is either pure bullshit or pure wrong."

"I almost feel sorry for you, brother." He opened the door. "Almost."

"Asshole."

A SILVER FORELEG pawed the ground sending dust into a whirlwind at his feet. He pawed again then snorted, moving closer to Evangeline, but stopped when he was

within a few yards. The horse was rippled with muscle—so cut and defined, he resembled a painting rather than a real horse. Evangeline opened her palm flat as a gesture of calm. He came closer, but instead of nuzzling her palm, he curled his right foreleg and lowered his body and head to her. How strange, she thought.

His eyes were so dark in the night, they appeared as black as coal—kind, not wild as she'd first thought. The horse stood straight and began to rub his lips over her palm. She raised her free hand to the horse's muzzle, rubbing in light circles around the silky area. "We finally meet. I knew you were real," she murmured to him.

She opened her mouth to speak again, and when her hand reach higher on his face, he vanished beneath her touch. "What the hell?" Evangeline twisted her body, looking frantically for the horse. Behind her, she heard his voice.

"Evangeline, Evangeline, come here. Come back to me. She turned to see Maverick gesturing to her as he stood at the end of the dirt path.

Evangeline woke—her gaze darting around the darkened room. She switched on the lamp on the table next to her bed. Sitting up, she rubbed her eyes before she visually swept the room in the dim light. "Damn, that seemed so real."

The clock read 3:45 AM. Even the night sounds had stilled. The silence consumed the room like a heavy blanket. She drew her legs to her chest and rested her chin upon her knees. She smiled when she remembered her date with Rick. For the first time in years, something had stirred in her. She wanted more, and when he'd placed a very chaste kiss on her forehead at her doorstep, at first, she'd been disappointed, but then a warmth embraced her. He wasn't going to push her. Maybe she should tell him everything. Maybe not. How about she enjoy what could happen and stop analyzing? Evangeline's jumbled thoughts revealed she wouldn't be getting any more sleep.

She threw back the quilt and reached for the jeans she'd worn to dinner and had thrown across the end of the bed. Socks, sneakers, and a hoodie were all she needed for a quick jaunt to the corral. Lately, watching Rick's new horse was one of her favorite things to do. Even though it was the middle of the night, she could try her own hand at making friends with the wary animal.

Walking down the dirt path, the darkness enveloped her, but in the distance, she followed the pale illumination the light kept on outside of the corral that was attached to a feed shed. Wait? Did she hear the whicker of not one, but two, horses? She knew Rick had planned to keep the horse away from the others until he was confident the abused animal had accepted him as a companion. She hurried her steps, careful to remain as quiet as possible.

Her hands flew to her mouth. There he was in corral standing next to the scrawny chestnut. All silver and black. He looked like a demon. The tip of his ebony tale brushed the ground, and his mane hung in waves. He was the most stunning animal she'd ever seen—and seen, she had, because she was perfectly sober on this night.

As she inched closer, she could see the ghost horse seeming to groom the other. The mare accepted his nuzzles and nibbles, but even Evangeline could tell the horse was tense from the attention. Her foot grazed a pebble, and she froze. So did the horses. The ghost horse jerked his head to where she stood, holding her breath. He trotted to the edge of the fence rail closest to her, snorting the entire way.

"Sorry," she whispered. "Go back to what you were doing. See?" she said, holding up her hands. "No phone, no recording. Your secret is safe with me."

He continued to snort and dance nervously in the corral. He raked his front hoof across the dirt twice, looked at her again, then sprinted across the corral and leaped over the rail—clearing the fence by a good eighteen inches. Evangeline ran to the fence to see if she could figure out where he was going, but he seemed to have vanished.

"Wasn't that somethin?" She said to the remaining horse. "You want to be friends?" She held out her flattened palm. "I don't have anything to offer other than a kind word. Whad'ya say?"

The horse eased herself to Evangeline, step by step, until she could extend her nose to Evangeline's palm. She sniffed and snuffled before getting close enough Evangeline could touch her muzzle.

"See? I'm not so bad. What do you think of your visitor? He's pretty hot. Don't you think? If I were you, I'd be all over that." The horse gave a low whicker.

"I know. I'm having my own man issues." She kicked the ground with her shoe. "Not so much an issue, but more of a 'what should I do' thing. I mean, I really like him, and I haven't had any feelings like that for years, especially in the last two. So, am I just desperate to get laid, or is there really something there? Then there's the whole 'I live in California... he lives here' thing. Although, truthfully, going back to California is getting less and less appealing. Functioning in society is getting less and less appealing, too. What if I just stayed up here amongst you horses? The people here don't nag you about getting on with your life. I'd have to have some sort of job. The money from the sale of the house will run out at some point. What do you think I should do, uh…you need a name."

She brushed her hand across the horse's forehead, circling the small patch of white. "How about Star? I'm going to call you Star. Well, Star, should I just throw caution to the wind and jump Maverick's bones? Or, should I play cool?"

Star stretched her head high and whinnied to the sky.

"So, you think I should go for it?"

CHAPTER EIGHT

Bleary-eyed but dressed, Evangeline trudged into the dining hall for breakfast. She'd purposely waited for the second breakfast, having decided that eating with the guests would be less uncomfortable than seeing Rick at the early breakfast. Despite her conversation with Star, Evangeline felt as though she'd lost some of her moxy after a couple hours sleep.

Why was this so hard? Well, probably because she'd only dated one man her entire life. She and Ian hadn't really dated. They'd grown up together and somehow ended up married. She scooped scrambled eggs onto her plate, dousing them in hot sauce and a sprinkle of cheddar cheese. She decided to cut down on the bacon and used tongs to pick out two of the savory slices instead of her usual four. She stacked sourdough toast and blackberry jam on top, so all she needed now was coffee. Regular, not decaf.

She managed to find an unoccupied table near the door of the dining hall and set her plate, utensils, and mug on the table. Her peace was short-lived as Lara and Rose slid onto the bench, one on each side of her, but no sign of Rick.

"So, how'd it go?" Lara hunched her shoulders and smiled.

"Fine. It went fine. How did you know we went out?" Her face heated as she tore a piece of toast and stuffed it in her mouth. Geez, she hated being the topic of gossip.

"Oh please," Lara scoffed. "He put on clean jeans, unscuffed boots and actually said hello to one of the guests. He was in a good mood, and you're the only one he's paid any attention to."

Evangeline gritted her teeth. "It went fine."

"Okay. You go out with Mav, and all you can say is 'fine.' What happened?" Lara leaned away from her and crossed her arms across her chest.

The fact that she'd fantasized the entire evening about what he looked like naked was not something she would relay to Lara or Rose. "We had a nice dinner. Talked. Listened to the band. I had a good time." She bit into the toast again and chewed after realizing how irritated they both became when she stopped talking. "Okay, I had a really good time. He's very nice."

Rose elbowed her. "And?"

"And he's very attractive." She licked a spot of jam that had wedged in the corner of her mouth. "So, if ya'll think he's so hot, why don't any of you make a claim?"

"We're related."

"Seriously? Is there anyone here who's not related? Is he your brother?" She choked and reached for her coffee.

"Except for the cowboys. They aren't related, but Rose, Dylan, and I are cousins to Mav and Keller," Lara said.

"When you goin' out again?" Rose asked.

"I don't know. Maybe we will. Maybe we won't." As good as the bacon looked in the dish, now her stomach roiled at the thought of the delicious grease sliding into her belly.

"Saturday is the first Ranch Dance," Lara smiled.

"Ranch Dance?" She was getting more nauseous by the minute.

"From May through October, once a month, we have a dance here. Local band. Great music though. It's open to the public. We get a pretty good crowd. A little dancing, a little drinking. Who knows?" Lara elbowed Evangeline from the other side.

"Somehow, I don't think Maverick is a dance kind of guy," Evangeline muttered.

"He's not, but if you're gonna be there, who knows? And it is on Saturday so he'll be done with work, and trail rides on Sunday don't start 'til noon. He won't have to help Keller unless we have a lot of people riding. Usually don't on Sundays this early in the season."

She'd been out of the game since she was twelve. Was this how things worked? "You know, I don't really have clothes for a dance. I came out here to ride and hike. I was just happy we basically went to a bar last night. I don't have dating clothes."

Rose put her arm around Evangeline's shoulder and pulled her closer. "It's not a prom. It's a country dance. As it happens, we're going into Deadwood today. There are some shops there with some really cute clothes. You don't need anything fancy."

She shoved the plate across the table. "Fine. I'm thirty…" she ran her hand across her mouth and mumbled, "years old. And you're treating this like a prom. Anyway, I could probably use some things. I'm tired of wearing the same five things every day."

EVANGELINE STUMBLED. Rose and Lara caught her

before she hit the ground with her bags. "Thank you. Although, giving me a Deadwood bar tour on an empty stomach wasn't the best idea. Can we get some food?"

They found a place to eat pizza and drink more beer.

"This town is so cool," Evangeline said. "Good thing I don't have a vehicle. I'd be here more often. I love places with a history, and this place is full of it."

"History, reputation, and the casinos are what bring in the tourists, which means money," Lara said as she took a bite of a slice of pepperoni. "A lot people think there's a certain romance here, but Deadwood has some very dark history to it. There's a whole after hours' tour of just how ugly things were."

"I suppose anywhere gold was in the equation it could get pretty bad." Evangeline surveyed the bags resting at her feet. "I have to admit, I've enjoyed buying some new things. I probably should've bought some of that perfume. It smelled nice. I should go back to that store."

"Honey, you don't need any perfume," Rose said. "Mav will sniff you out anywhere."

Lara shot Rose the evil eye, and Evangeline wrinkled her nose at the image of Rick sniffing around like a dog. "I'm ready to go. How about you guys?"

"Yeah, we've got to get back to start dinner." Lara gathered their empty paper plates and tossed them into a nearby trash container. They left the beer mugs on the table and a few bucks for the server.

All were quiet on the way back to the ranch. Evangeline was sleepy and decided to use the time before dinner to catch a nap.

ALTHOUGH VERY UNLIKE HERSELF, Evangeline skipped dinner. She wasn't sure if the unease in her stomach was the euphoria of a great date, worry if he didn't think it was a great date, or the excess of alcohol she'd consumed earlier in the day.

Instead, she wandered down the path to the corral to visit Star. She found Star and Rick. He was brushing her matted and dirty hair—dropping handfuls of winter hair to the ground. Star didn't seem too upset with his hands on her, but she still sidestepped his touch on occasion.

"She's looking so much better than when I first saw her. Do you think she'll be okay?" Evangeline smiled as the horse whinnied a welcome to her.

He never looked up but continued the long strokes on the horse's haunches. "Hard to say right now if she'll ever be a good trail horse. She might get to where she's okay around groups of people and horses at the same time. If not, I'll take her to the sanctuary." He paused, and they locked eyes. "Everyone deserves a second chance in life. Don't you think?"

"Yes, they do. Can I come in? Star and I sorta had a chat last night, and I think she likes me." Evangeline waited for Rick to motion her inside.

"Star, huh?"

"Well, I didn't hear you call her anything, and I thought she needed a name." She unlocked the gate and swung it open, careful to relock it when she was fully inside the corral.

"Star's a good name."

She advanced upon the pair and extended her hand for Star to sniff and then nuzzle. "I went to the late breakfast this morning. I guess I wasn't sure if… you know…if it would be awkward after our date last night."

He stopped brushing and rested his forearms on the horse's back. Star started to move but calmed herself and remained quiet under his arms.

"I see you're skipping dinner," he said, one dark brow arching. "Is that related to me or our date last night?"

Deflect and defend. Well, that wasn't fair. Her nose tickled from the hair and dust she'd just inhaled with her deep breath. Fine, then she would lay it all out. "Look, I haven't had a date in a while. I mean, like in over two decades. I may not be the best judge of how to gauge a good date. When I got back, I felt pretty good, and I really liked spending the time with you...but then, you disappeared all day, and now I'm not so sure."

She rubbed her hands across her face and stepped back from Star. "God, now I feel really stupid."

Rick nudged his dusty cowboy hat up higher on his head. "Did it ever occur to you that I might have the same concerns? Or having a job might be part of why I wasn't on your radar today?"

She couldn't breathe. A rock or chunk of surprise had lodged in her throat. "Oh. Really?"

A raised eyebrow and half smile from across the horse allowed her to take a breath.

He handed her the brush, and she began the task of de-shedding on her side of Star. She used light strokes so as not to upset the horse, but even so, hair came out in clumps. She wondered if this horse had ever been brushed.

"I stay away from ranch guests. It's really a bad idea and can be bad for business." He began finger-combing the tangles in Star's mane. "But you, I tried but couldn't get you out of my head. There's a lot we don't know about each other, and for now, that's okay. Can we just enjoy the time and see where it goes?"

Every nerve and muscle in her body let out a collective sigh of relief, and brushing Star became a loving task as opposed to a distraction from a possible rejection. "I'm not opposed to that at all. I'm pretty rusty."

"Shall I oil you up?" A grin spread across his face.

Evangeline scanned her surroundings. "Well, probably not here. The dirt and all. Pretty messy."

He raised his chin in agreement. "I could cook you a hotdog later."

"There's no bonfire tonight, is there?"

"No, but I have a fire pit, hotdogs, and maybe could snatch a few marshmallows from the kitchen."

MAVERICK WAITED until he had the fire going before changing out of his clothes covered in horse hair and washing his hands free of old log soot from the fire pit. He grabbed the open package of hot dogs, half a package of buns, mustard, and relish and carried them to the gathering of cut up tree trunks serving as seats around the fire pit he shared with his family. The clearing on the hill above the ranch hall served as the unofficial setting for family meetings. Far enough from the guest rooms their conversations would not be overheard, but close enough if trouble arose.

He heard a huffing ascending the hill and smiled. Few people wanted to navigate the steep path up to where the Silver family cabins rested. The older he got, the more he appreciated the separation from the real world.

"Are you okay?" he asked when he saw her appear.

"Gee fuckin' whiz. You have to do that every day?" She bent over and rested her hands on her knees. Wheezing but still grasping a bag of marshmallows.

"Sometimes two or three times a day. If you do it enough, it gets easier. Thanks for bringing the marshmallows."

"Lara caught me as I was coming up and said you called her." She straightened and finished the last few steps. "Called her, as opposed to going down and getting them yourself."

"If it isn't absolutely necessary to walk down the hill, then why do it?" He reached for her hand and led her to a tree seat before taking the marshmallows. "Would you like anything? Beer, whiskey, water, soda...oxygen?"

"All of the above, except soda. Never soda, again."

Puzzled by her last statement, Maverick didn't respond but went inside and returned with two beers and two bottles of water. He handed her one of each and set his on the adjoining stump. He went to the woodpile and returned with a branch devoid of leaves. Reaching into his back pocket, he pulled out a Swiss Army knife and began sharpening one end of the branch to a point.

"I could have brought up hot dog sticks, too."

"This is a hot dog stick. Here." He handed her the stick and motioned to the hotdogs on one of the stumps.

She slipped two from the package and speared them onto the stick. As he watched her progress, a smile came to his face. He'd been smiling a lot lately.

She frowned at him. "What? One's for you."

"Well, thank you." Popping the cap off his beer, he drew a long drink. "What's the thing with soda? I mean, it's not a big deal if you don't like it. It's not good for you, but when you said it, the word came out like it was vile in your mouth."

Evangeline extended the stick over the fire in silence. Only the popping of the wood cracked the heaviness.

"I'm sorry. You don't need to answer. Brings up

an unpleasant thought I'm guessing, and it's none of my business."

Evangeline rotated the dogs until every part was whistling and bubbling but not burned. Maverick wrapped a bun around each one when she pulled the stick from the flames. She set the stick on the ground and squirted mustard on the one he gave her.

"I'll tell you."

He plastered mustard and relish on his hotdog before setting beside her. "Really, you don't have to."

Evangeline held onto her dinner and stared into the fire. "When I said my husband died...it was complicated. It's kinda strange, and explaining is hard. Ian...my husband...and I grew up together. We'd lived next door to each other since we were both four-years-old. Played together, went to school. When my dad left, Ian was there for me. Everyone always said how cute we were. In high school, we made the natural progression as a couple. We were made for each other, everyone said. We went to the same college, and when we graduated, everyone assumed we'd get married because we were perfect for each other. And we did. Perfect little wedding cake topper couple."

Maverick watched her as she spoke. He knew something heartbreaking was coming.

"Thing is, Ian and I had spent so much of our lives together, we were more like brother and sister. I think both of us were afraid to disappoint everyone else, so we stayed married. In some aspects, we were great together. We had similar life views. We liked a lot of the same things, but we could never be married in the way a couple should be married. I knew him so well that I noticed his attraction to someone he worked with. He never acted on it. I knew that, too, but I thought Ian and I both deserved happiness in all ways, and I told him to ask this woman out. He wouldn't do it because we were married. I finally said we needed to divorce to make us both happy."

She bit into the hotdog, chewing slowly and seeming to savor the fire-kissed meal. "It was going to be so easy. Sell the house, split everything up. We both had good jobs. No alimony, just a simple, amicable divorce. He was coming over to the house —I hadn't moved out yet—to get more of his stuff, and then we were going to go sign the papers. He called and said he was on his way, and I asked him to stop and get me a soda."

A tear escaped her moist eye and trickled down the curve of her cheek. "He stopped at a convenience stop and walked in on a robbery. Guy shot him point blank in the head. So, by technicality, I got everything…house, cars, insurance money."

She began to shake. Her hotdog spilled out of her hands onto the dirt. Maverick watched, helpless to change her past.

"So, because of my selfish request, a good man, *a very good man*, never got to have real love. And I got tired of people telling me I needed to move on. That it wasn't my fault. So, I moved out of my life and ended up here." She inhaled a deep sniff, but the dribble from her nose did not budge.

Maverick handed her a bandana and his hotdog. He tossed Evangeline's into the fire, and the smell of burning meat swirled in the smoke. "Here, wipe and eat. I won't tell you to get over it or move on. You will when you can and want to. We all grieve differently. I'm sure I'd feel the same way. You sure did travel a long way to 'get away,' though."

She wiped the snot and bit into the hot dog. Relish and mustard dribbled down her chin. "Wasn't a complete accident." She wiped the yellow-green mess and took another bite.

"What do ya mean?" He was a little hungry, too, but resisted the urge to roast another. He wanted to hear her answer.

"A few years ago, my mom gave me a box of things my dad had left. She never said much about his leaving, and I never asked. It was very mysterious between them, a lot. Anyway, in the box was a brochure for the Silver Spear Ranch. I don't remember him ever saying anything or coming here, but the pictures were pretty, and something about what I was seeing drew me here. I haven't been disappointed."

"Here," she handed him the remaining half of the hotdog he gave her. "This was not my intent for the evening. I'm sorry."

"So what was your intent?" He grinned as he shoved the rest into his mouth.

"Not that."

Her scarlet face added heat to his own want, which was catching fire. The first day she'd arrived, he'd noticed her. She gave off a scent only a few would ever catch. From the moment he'd recognized the familiar aroma, fighting to stay away from her had proved futile. When he'd watched her sit a horse, he'd nearly collapsed with need. Oh, how he wanted her to ride him with her legs wrapped around his middle, squeezing and telling him with only her legs what she wanted. Evangeline, even with her tear-stained face shattered his resolve.

"Well, I mean…" She fumbled, and her face grew redder.

"Another time. Marshmallow?"

CHAPTER NINE

The free flowing cream-colored skirt and hunter green tank she'd purchased on her trip to Deadwood served a few purposes. They weren't so western, she couldn't wear them anywhere, and with all the riding and reining she'd been doing, the tank showed off her emerging biceps. The riding hadn't helped one bit to strengthen her for trudging up the hill to Rick's place, however.

After dinner on dance night, she helped set up for the night's entertainment. Since she'd spilled her guts to him the other night, she'd made herself a little scarce. Evangeline had watched him from the top rail of the corral working with Star. He'd also said little during those times, but he was focused on the horse, and she was focused on watching his seemingly innate way with gaining the horse's trust and preparing her for a life away from abuse. They talked, but mostly the safe inane chit chat people shared who aren't sure what to say for fear of revealing true feelings.

After everything was ready and people who weren't ranch guests began to arrive, Evangeline sidled up to the bar and asked Dylan for a whiskey. "Is this for fun, or is it a moneymaker?"

Dylan poured her glass and presented it with a grin. "When people dance, they get thirsty. They buy drinks. The drinks make 'em happy, and they buy more drinks."

"Then why do you only do this once a month?" The amber liquid made a sweet burn in her throat.

"Then it's not special."

The band began to play a country pop hit. Couples hurried to the dance floor—one side formed for line dancing, while others two-stepped with their partners. "Let the drinking begin." Evangeline raised her glass to Dylan but kept an eye on the door.

"Don't worry, he'll be here." Lara's whispered message in her ear gave her a start.

"I wasn't looking for Maverick."

"Of course not." Lara threw back her head and laughed before taking her tray of bowls crammed with peanuts to the tables lining the perimeter of the room.

Of course she was.

She didn't have to wait long before the door opened and inside stepped the man who'd infiltrated her dreams and didn't judge her departure from life. In that moment, she realized that never in her life had she had the opportunity for a man to strip her of oxygen without even touching her. Rick was the poster cowboy for women's wet dreams. Dressed in dark Wranglers, a pristine white western-style shirt, and a black Resistol sans dust, Rick Cambios-Plata's appearance set Evangeline on fire.

She swallowed and attempted to sip her whiskey with the casualness of passing the peanuts as he approached, but her shaky hand forced her to set the glass on the bar. The loud thump made her wince.

"Well, whad'ya know, you do have legs." He nodded to her bare calves.

"And you have a clean shirt."

He laughed, snatched her hand in his, and maneuvered his way through the crowd of dancers.

"You didn't even ask me if I wanted to dance...or even could dance." Her protest was weak at best, especially after he placed his hand on the small of her back and pulled her close.

"Do you? Can you? Does it even matter?"

She craned her neck to catch the mischief in his eyes. "Yes. Sort of. And no."

Her *sort of* became a quick no when he expertly two-stepped her across the floor. She would've been better off standing on his boots. When the song ended, the band changed the beat to a slow romantic ballad. The pace suited her much better than the previous one, and through the intimacy of their bodies, Evangeline absorbed the heat radiating from his chest.

He stopped dancing and broke the connection. "Come on."

"What's wrong?"

"Too many eyes."

Evangeline glanced around the room and saw what he was referring to. Rose, Lara, and Dylan all stood at the bar with cheesy grins plastered on their faces.

Rick led her outside onto the path in the direction of the barn, but when they arrived at the barn, he kept going beyond the line of the fence until they reached a collection of boulders. Evangeline knew the place. The way the rocks stood offered a natural crevasse large enough for bodies to pass. She'd spent time reading in the shelter—a stone nook perfect for being alone.

Lights from the outside of the barn, and more

from the ranch hall, illuminated the area with a smoky glow. Music from the band wafted through the breeze and mixed with the sounds of the night. Evangeline's skin pimpled, but the chilly night air wasn't enough to cool her heated body on the inside.

"What are we going to do out here?" She rested her back against a rock and cocked her head to the side in false innocence. Maybe she could flirt.

"Talk." His dark eyes were darker, larger and full of lust. He couldn't possibly mean talk. He extended his arm above her head, bracing it against the rock. His body now hovered like a drone. A faint woodsy fragrance balanced between them, but he still held the sweet aroma of hay and horses—something she'd never tired of.

"I see. This," she glanced around the rocky enclosure, "is a perfect place for…talking."

"When you told me about what happened to your husband, I don't think I said the right things. I should have said more."

She fought the tears threatening to gather in her eyes. She'd cried enough in the last two years. "You know, people have said a lot of things to me since it happened. I know they meant well, but I really think what they were saying was more for their own benefit. Telling me not to feel guilty, to get back out there, and move on with my life. You said three sentences and not one of those things were in those words. For the first time, someone told me what I really needed to hear, and that was you."

He gave a slight nod. "Okay."

"Was that the only reason we came out here?" Her boldness surprised her. Was she moving on?

He placed his other hand over her head on the boulder. "I want to kiss you without an audience. Is that okay?"

"The kiss or the audience?" She really was beginning to understand this flirting thing.

His teeth were white in the darkness. Then, Evangeline did something she'd never done before in her life. She wrapped her arms around his neck and pulled his face to hers until their lips joined. The groan from deep in his throat made her want more, and she pushed her tongue into his mouth to feel the fire inside of him. He grabbed her by the waist, pulling her so close Evangeline thought she'd moved inside of him.

She kissed him like she was starving. She was. She was starving for a physical connection she'd never had with Ian. She was thirty-five years old, and yet, in some ways, she was still a virgin. Here were the shivers, the aching between her legs, the wetness she feared would travel down her thighs. She was suffocating in the most glorious fashion, and if she died from lack of air, then death couldn't be any sweeter.

Much to her dismay, Rick broke the kiss, but his smile and hungry eyes told her not for long.

"Your skills are not limited to horseback," he said.

"I'm wondering if I have a lot of skills, I've never used," she said, brushing his cheek with her hand.

"My money is on yes." His hand slid to the hem of her skirt, and instinctively she raised her leg and braced it against the side of his thigh. Evangeline was grateful she'd decided to shave her legs for only the fourth time since she'd arrived. Either she'd anticipated or fantasized about his calloused hand brushing her skin, but either way, the coarse massage made her shudder.

"You okay?"

A not so subtle shudder she found out. "I'm more than okay." A flick of her hand, and Rick's hat tumbled from his head, giving her full access to the dense waves of his chocolate hair. He moaned again and pressed her further back against the boulder. His lips were a sharp contrast to his rough hands, but she fell into a deep spell, craving more of his rugged touch.

His hand moved higher on her leg and, oh so close, to an opening unexplored for years. She encircled her leg behind his waist, unsure if her other leg would continue to hold up her flaming body. Every movement of Rick's lips on her neck and the crest of her breast was pulling down a zipper to reveal a world she'd only dreamed of. Ian and she had sex... at first, but in reality, being intimate with him became icky. He was so much like a brother to her that intercourse had seemed wrong. Now, plastered against a hard rock with Rick's rock-hard dick on the other side of those jeans, was mind numbing. It wreaked havoc on a body that hadn't had an orgasm in years.

She fumbled with one hand to undo his belt, but the jeans were another matter. Reluctantly, she removed her other hand from his hair and went to work on the button. He moaned with every riffle of her fingers, and her confidence grew tenfold.

When she managed to undo the button and as she fingered the zipper, Rick reached his arm around his back. He flashed a condom packet in front of her.

Evangeline laughed. "You know, at this moment, I don't even care. I have a feeling this is about to be the best fuck I've ever had, and I don't care if it comes with a doctor visit. I'm willing to risk it all for five minutes of heaven."

Even in the dark, she could see his eyebrows rise.

"Five minutes?"

"Just throwing a number out there. I don't know. I have a birth control implant. Not sure why, but I do. So it wouldn't be that type of doctor visit." She brushed his cheek. "You were pretty confident, weren't you?"

"I was more like pretty hopeful," Rick said as he rolled her tank up her waist. His rough hands were tender in their motion but determined in their path. When the shirt reached her bra, Evangeline let go of him and ripped the top over her head. She'd had the forethought to buy a bra that didn't say "granny" all over it. Nothing too special but navy lace with a lacy T-back.

"You are glorious," he said as he lowered his lips to hers. In the midst of his tongue ravaging her mouth, he'd pulled his underwear down enough that his cock sprang forward, slapping Evangeline's hand. She wound her fingers around the shaft and felt his body shudder.

"I don't want to…I can't wait anymore. I want to feel you inside of me." Her breaths were ragged and trembled with anticipation.

She heard a rip of paper and opened her eyes to see Rick pulling the condom over his cock. It was every bit as impressive as it had felt in her hand.

"Wrap your arms around my neck again and your legs around my waist," he said. "I'll hold you tight."

He barely had the words out of his mouth before Evangeline anchored herself to him. His body heat simmered through her skin, warming the wetness coating her thighs. She marveled at his strength in holding her, but the trembling of her body had nothing to do with her fear of falling but rather her ability to accept all of him.

"I've gotcha. Don't worry."

His clutched and squeezed her ass, it hurt for a moment, until the pain turned to intense pleasure. His fingers were like steel poles impaling her, but she'd wear the bruises with a secret smile. The pulsating response of her ass distracted her until she felt his cock ready to enter.

"That's what I'm worried about," she whispered.

"What?" His voice was low and sexy.

"That I can't take..." she swallowed, "all of you."

The touch of his lips on her ear sent an involuntary gasp through her whole body. He nuzzled again and said. "We'll go slow, however painful it may be for me. I want inside of you so bad my dick's trying leave my body."

With each modest push, Evangeline relaxed, ready to accept more of him. Her fears fled; replaced by an insatiable craving of him. When her body opened fully and housed him snug inside, she'd never experienced such total possession. One more deep breath and… "Hey, what are you doing?" Empty. He'd pulled out, but her angst was short-lived as his calloused finger caressed her nub.

"Oh, fuck me," she moaned.

He snickered. "I'm tryin', darling."

With each stroke, Evangeline found a new part of herself—eager, willing, and oh so sexy. As the waves of her shudders began, she found herself stuffed full of Rick. Her moans changed to screams, and he covered her mouth with his own, groaning as his body convulsed into hers.

They slid to the mossy ground with Rick cradling her back. "Well, that was the best part of my day," he murmured.

He kissed her again, and Evangeline relaxed in his arms as she lay against his chest. "Best part of my life," she mumbled.

"What'd you say?"

"Nothing."

His arms squeezed tighter, warming her against the cool breeze picking up through the trees. "I heard you. Things like that could give a guy a big head."

Evangeline jerked her head toward the sound of excited whinnying. "Are you hearing that? Sounds like they're loose…like it's coming from the hill."

"Sound travels strange out here."

"No," Evangeline shoved off his chest with her head cocked listening in the dark. "I hear hooves. More than one set. There's horses out there loose."

As she started to rise, she found herself flat against Rick's chest. "It's nothing," he said. "The way the canyon is, the sounds from the corral are like they're right next to you."

"Okay. Seems weird." She rested her head against his chest. How odd his heart beat so slowly. After their "best sex she ever had," she could count time between his beats while hers threatened to explode. "You're heart beat is so slow."

"Always been that way. Freak of nature, I suppose." He raked his fingers through her hair, sending more erotic sensations through her body.

As much as she was enjoying resting on top of him, she didn't believe he could be comfortable on the ground. "You want to go back to the dance?"

His massage of her hair had lulled her into a sense of deep euphoria. Going back to the dance was not something she wanted to do.

"I'd rather have a tooth pulled than spend any time at those dances. I only came because of you. We can go inside though. I feel the goose bumps on your skin. You must be getting cold," he said.

"We could go to my cabin." She placed her ear above his heart to see if the beats had picked up.

Slower, they were much slower. How weird. That wasn't even human.

"Sorry, there's a no staff in guests' cabins rule, unless you're housekeeping."

"Isn't this your ranch? I mean partly yours?"

"Would it be fair to have rules only for certain people?" He rolled her to the ground and sat up. "Now, going to my cabin falls under a completely different category."

Evangeline studied the velvety ground in the dark, hoping to find the underwear thrown from her body without any regard for finding it in the dark. "I can't find my underwear. Maybe, I'll just leave it."

"Your name's not labeled in the back is it?"

"Not since summer camp when I was ten." She caught a contrast of color on Rick's black boot. "Oh, wait, it's wrapped around your boot." She snatched the lacy blue garment from the tip of his boot and stuffed it in the pocket of her skirt.

"So, are we going to roast hot dogs again?"

As he stood, he pulled her with him. "I might be putting one dog in the oven."

CHAPTER TEN

Maverick carried the saddle from the tack room to the line of horses tied at the corral rails. He clucked to Sparky, an Appaloosa, to alert the horse he was there. Sparky was getting old, but even as a younger horse, the gelding had little git up and go, and so, the cowboys working at the ranch at the time began calling him Sparky. Maverick liked the horse. Despite his propensity for being lazy, Sparky was gentle and good with young children. He was tall enough the kids thought they were riding a much more spirited animal, but with a disposition that allowed him to accept the ineptitude of young inexperienced kids with ease.

Squeezing between Sparky and the bay Keller was saddling, Maverick tossed the saddle blanket over the horse's back before gently settling the saddle in place.

"You seem to have an unusually genuine cheerfulness about you this morning." Keller removed the halter of the horse he stood beside and slipped a bridle over the animal's nose. "I take it last night went well...?"

"It was fine, but I wasn't alone." He pulled the girth on Sparky's saddle tight.

"What ya gonna do? They're young?" Keller wrapped the loose reins around the aluminum rail before stepping to the back of the horse and giving the bay a light slap on its haunches. "You should have known at least Lara and Rose would be eavesdropping in disguise? I don't think Dylan gives a rat's ass unless he's the one getting some."

"We moved to my cabin." Maverick pushed his knee into Sparky's side. The old horse was notorious for holding his breath when the girth was tightened. The horse took a breath, and Maverick pulled the slack tight on the girth.

"And?" Keller's smile spread wide across his face.

"And, fuck you." With a pat on the neck, Maverick left Sparky and headed to the barn.

"You know what I mean," Keller yelled after him.

Yes, he did know what his brother meant. One

night together wasn't long enough to build trust. Spilling his secrets now would very likely end their budding relationship. Truth was, he was afraid. Evangeline evoked feelings he'd never wanted to admit he had. Straddling this tightrope was hard. Being a loner wasn't what he wanted, but South Dakota wasn't exactly the center of the universe, and finding the one who fit and understood him was about as easy as winning the lottery. Someone would win, but odds were it wouldn't be you. He had so many responsibilities: the ranch, his family, Storm Canyon. If one failed, they all did.

Every year seemed to bring everyone in the canyon closer to a world they didn't want. Mirran Ranch had been family-owned at one time, but a corporation took advantage of their financial struggle, and now, the once quaint and rustic getaway was a haven for those whose idea of getting away from it all was a sprawling indoor gym, track, and pool. Also bringing servers, who brought guests froufrou drinks and packed gourmet lunches for their flatland trail rides on horses who probably wished they were dead.

He wouldn't let anyone but family handle Silver Spear Ranch. Even as his mom and dad were reaching the age where they had to make a major decision, Maverick had already decided he'd die before someone else had their name on the ranch. One decision down and a major one to go.

He'd checked the book and didn't see Evangeline's name down for any rides today. Perhaps she'd be hiking or up at the other corral watching him work with Star. As he thought of her brushing Star, his cock hardened. She had her own way with horses. Which made complete sense.

If he hurried, he could catch her at breakfast. Smiling as he made his way up the path to the dining hall, Maverick envisioned what he would see upon entering. Evangeline unapologetically eating a small stack and a pile of scrambled eggs with bacon. That woman did love her food. He loved how when he touched her, her curves melted in his hand. If he continued the fantasy, he would get little done today other than having Evangeline naked and giving his cock the ride of its life.

There she was sitting at the end of one of the long tables drowning an unsuspecting pancake, or what was left of one, in syrup. She wore a Dodgers baseball cap with her hair dangling through the opening in the cap. She was without the makeup she'd worn last night but still looked fresh and beautiful.

He filled his plate and joined her. "Mornin'."

Evangeline set down her fork, sipped and swallowed hot coffee from her mug, and said, "You just got up and left me this morning. No 'bye', 'had a good time', or even a 'kiss my ass.' It's a little weird to wake up in someone else's bed alone."

"It was four-thirty, and considering we'd only been sleeping maybe two hours, I thought I'd let you sleep. If I'd wanted you to leave, I'd have said so." His pointed gaze normally stopped people in their tracks, but not her.

"Well, maybe next time, you could wake me and give me a kiss." She picked up her fork and continued eating the now soggy pancake.

Inside his heart leaped. "So, there'll be a next time?"

"Well, if it were up to me, there'd be an *all the time*."

Her coy smile made his crotch uncomfortable. "I have to work."

She shrugged. "There is that."

"There is an 'I'll be done by three today.'" She never broke eye contact. Now, he was the one a little intimidated. She was magnificent.

"Keller asked me to go on the noon trail ride." She bounced her fork between her thumb and forefinger. "He said a couple of cowboys are off today. Why don't you go?"

Fuck that. He could deal with people on a superficial basis, but some of the guests who went on the rides made him want to escape to Storm Canyon permanently. Keller and the rest of the family had nixed his idea that only horse people could go on trail rides. They'd agreed that such a decree could decrease the stupid level exponentially, but trail rides, even by idiots, were one of their biggest income generators. While most of the stupid wasn't dangerous, it was beyond what he could he handle.

"We have an agreement. Only in extreme emergencies will I lead a ride. By extreme emergency, I mean, the line of succession is the cowboys, Keller, Dylan, Lara, Rose, and then me. I'm not really good for business."

Evangeline scraped the few remaining bits of scrambled eggs from her plate. "Okay, so, I go on the nooner. Get back, grab somethin' to eat, shower and, by three, I could be around, wine glass in hand ready to uh…talk maybe…" She laughed. "Who'm I kidding. You're not a big talker."

He leaned in. His frame crossed the table into her space. "You don't need to shower."

Ever so slight, but he saw it. He saw the slow twitch of her jaw as she swallowed. He smiled to himself. She'd flinched and didn't even know it.

"Well, then." He stood and tipped his baseball cap. "Here's hoping to see you and your glass of wine."

EVANGELINE HUSTLED Baxter to the front of the line alongside Keller, who was leading the noon ride. Baxter loved to be in front, and he needed little urging to pick up the pace and pass the other horses on the wide spot on the trail where Evangeline chose to move ahead.

"So, did you know this was a group of Class A assholes when you invited me on this ride?" She spoke low in Spanish, knowing Keller was also bilingual.

"*Si. Lo siento.*" He flashed her a cheesy smile.

"You're not sorry, you ass."

He continued the conversation in Spanish. "I know they're fuck wads. They come every year on a corporate teambuilding weekend. The ones who aren't jerks don't come on the ride."

"Hey," came a booming voice, "speaka da English, or I'll have to call Immigration." Evangeline turned and recognized the voice of the biggest ass of all of them...the one who'd been riding right in front of her.

Her blood boiled. "You may have to listen to their

shit, but I don't." She reined Baxter to trot back to the man.

She eyed the stick he'd snapped from an overhanging branch. "Maybe if you'd learned to speak another language, you'd know what we were talking about. Then again, maybe you wouldn't want to know."

"I don't have to. I'm an American." He looked down to his mount. "Goddam horse is as lazy as you people."

"The horse responds to the ability of the rider."

"I could get you fired." He glared at her.

She scoffed as Baxter danced, sensing her growing anger. "I don't fuckin' work here. You can't do shit to me." She leaned closer. "I'll tell you what though. If Sparky is not a suitable horse for you, maybe your skills are better suited to Baxter here."

"Evangeline…" Keller's voice held a warning. She held up her hand to silence him.

"I saw you marked on the list that you're an expert horseman. It was probably an honest mistake they gave you Sparky." She dismounted. "Here, take Baxter."

The man's chest rose and fell in a nervous fashion. His stare went from Evangeline to his colleagues. "Sure, I'd prefer to ride a horse with a little life left in him."

He dismounted and handed the reins to Evangeline as she did the same. Baxter was at least two hands taller than the gelding, and she had to bite her lip to keep from laughing as the man struggled to mount the powerful horse.

"Are we ready?" Keller called. "We have an open space ahead where we can speed up a little."

The group began walking again, and Evangeline knew she felt a little too much self-satisfaction as she watched the asshole struggling with Baxter who was walking but walking sideways and tossing his head in the air. *This won't last long.*

As they entered the clearing, Keller told the riders they were going to pick up the pace and urged his mount to a canter. The others followed suit, laughing at themselves as they adjusted to the pace. Baxter, however, was still side-stepping, and the man smacked him on the ass with the stick. She sat wide-eyed on Sparky as Baxter bucked and bolted, and the man executed a perfect gainer in the air before hitting the ground in a thud on his backside. Keller caught Baxter's reins and stopped the horse while the other riders seemed, at first, horrified then tickled at their colleague's misfortune.

"Mother fucker." The man groaned and wheezed as he lay flat on the dirt.

Keller handed Baxter's reins off to Evangeline as

he passed by. He never dismounted but leaned a few inches over the man. "Are you hurt? Can you walk?"

The man sat up, inhaled a deep breath, and said. "I'm okay. I can get up." Small groans escaped his mouth in his effort to stand. "Maybe I'll take the other horse."

"No," Keller said, "what you will do is walk your ass down the trail back to the ranch. These horses are too valuable to have assholes like you mistreating them."

Evangeline nodded when Keller motioned her to ride Baxter.

The man brushed the dust from his jeans and stepped toward Keller. "You can't do that—make me walk back."

"I can, and I will. Don't be too embarrassed. You're not the first asshole who's had to hike back."

Huffing, the man pointed a finger at Keller. "I'll talk to the barn boss about you."

"I am the fuckin' boss."

"Then I'll talk to the owner...that big dude who doesn't speak to anyone."

Keller shook his head. "He's not the owner, and I'm doing you a favor and suggest you not, mention this to Maverick. However, you are more than welcome to speak with Jim or Betty."

He turned and began scuffing the dirt as he stomped away. "See if we return here again."

"You're breakin' my heart."

"Any other of you assholes want to join him? If I see another stick used on an animal, I'll beat your asses with it."

Evangeline could visibly see the others gulp and quickly shake their heads. "You want me to take Sparky back?"

"Naw, just turn him loose. He'll head back to barn himself. I'll call Maverick and tell him to expect him."

Once they returned to the barn, her first thought was to shower to wash away the sweat and trail dust, but then she remembered Rick's comment. She'd at least wash her face, and after grinding bits of dirt between her teeth, she decided to brush those as well.

The incident between her and the man still irritated her—not because of the immigration comment. She'd heard that plenty of times in her life. Some thought it funny and harmless, while others were just plain mean. She'd stopped letting that bother her years ago. You couldn't change narrow-minded asses. There was always ten ready to take their place. What bothered her was when people had such little regard for animals. Horses had been her salvation when her father had left without explanation. Maybe he'd explained. He'd left her a letter, but she'd never read it. Still sealed in the envelope, the letter was stuck inside the pamphlet for the ranch. She'd brought both with her for some unknown reason. Maybe her subconscious mind was telling her the letter needed to be read.

On the outside of the corral where Star lived was a small aluminum shed holding feed and tack. Behind the shed was an overhang where they stored bales of hay for the horses housed in this corral. Evangeline had changed into shorts, put on her dressy cowboy boots, poured a glass of red wine, and made herself somewhat comfortable on a bale of hay. Even with longer shorts, wayward straws still poked through her shorts and the back of her thighs.

Footsteps approached, but from the sound she knew Rick was not the one walking her way. When the source of the steps rounded the corner, she almost dropped her glass. The asswipe from the ride didn't seemed shocked to find her there.

"Sitting on your throne?" He crossed his arms over his chest and sank his weight on one leg.

Well, he was still pissed, so she decided to continue to be the source. "*Si, la corte está in sessión pare los idiotas masculinos.*"

His flushed face became redder as he shifted

from one foot to the other. "You're a smug little bitch, aren't you?"

A sip of wine kept her from laughing. *"Sí, bastante. Pero es la gente come tú quienes hacen que todo esto valga la peña. Sin embargo, te daré una chance para redimirte. Hay alguna razón por la cual no debas ser tildado come un fanático de mente pequeña?"*

"God dammit! Stop it!" He stepped toward her.

Evangeline glanced at her now empty wine glass. She supposed she could break the glass against the metal wall and use it as a weapon.

"I'd highly suggest you move yourself away from her."

At the sound of Rick's voice, relief poured over her. Evangeline sought to calm her racing heart with deep breaths. She'd seen him approaching but hadn't said anything. As nervous as she was, she wanted to see the man's reaction to Rick's element of surprise, knowing it would be worth it.

The man turned, and when he locked gazes with Rick, he stumbled backward from the shed. "I can't believe this place would tolerate guests harassing other guests."

Evangeline became a spectator of the show. She set the glass on a bale of hay and pulled up her knees. Oh, if she only had popcorn. Rick could be intimidating as hell on any normal day, but now, he was downright hair-raising and sexy as all get out. She brushed the feathery hairs standing on her forearm.

"We don't," Rick said. "So, you can head out as soon as you get your stuff packed."

The man straightened, and his jaw dropped. "You can't do that."

"As head of security, I can."

"But...bu..."

Evangeline chuckled, watching the man trying to puff himself up.

"I...I want a fu...full refund," he stammered.

"Are you fucking kidding me?" Rick advanced on the man, who quickly seemed to lose his nerve. "You've got two hours to get your shit and get out."

The man tripped and fell backward on the ground. "We came as a group. I don't have any way of leaving."

He's going to have one sore ass, Evangeline thought.

Rick extended his hand to the man whose bluster had deflated at rapid speed. "The way I see it, you can call an Uber, or either Keller or I, will drive you to the airport in Rapid City."

"I'll call an Uber." He accepted Rick's assistance but, once on his feet, he made a hasty retreat down the path to the cabins.

"You aren't head of security. You don't even have

security here." She marveled at how fast his expression changed from menacing to jocular.

"He doesn't know that. Besides, the safety of the guests does fall partly on me. I'm the biggest dude here, you know. Are you okay?" He brushed her cheek with the back of his hand, sending a shiver up and down her body.

"I'm fine. I'd already figured out how I was going to defend myself before you walked up." She kissed his cheek. "But, I'm glad you did. Creepy guy."

"Keller told me what happened on the ride, and then I saw him walking up the path. He must have seen you going that way. I'm a little sorry, he backed down. I would have enjoyed beating his ass into the ground, although my money would've been on you. I particularly liked the part where you called him a small-minded bigot."

She wrinkled her nose. "So, you heard me?"

"Every word. Let's see. 'Court was in session for jerks of the male species, and I'll give yourself a chance to redeem yourself. Any reason you shouldn't be tagged as a…small-minded bigot?' Yeah, I enjoyed it. However, you are not a smug little bitch, and you have no idea how much I wanted to ram my fist into his throat."

Rick eased her backwards step by step until her back flattened against the metal of the shed. His hands slid her arms over her head and pinned them high. Both of her wrists fit into the grip of one of his hands. With his other hand, he pushed the spaghetti strap of her shirt from her shoulder and planted kisses along the plane of her shoulder to the curve of her neck. With each kiss, he inhaled, and his hot breath on each exhale made her clench everything her body could clench before low moans born in her throat traveled and released through her lips.

"You didn't shower," he mumbled as he continued kissing across her neck to her other shoulder.

"No, I did not. However, I do find it a little odd you get turned on by the smell of sweat, dirt, and horses."

"Odd enough you want me to stop?"

She tried moving her hands to feel the ripples of his biceps peeking out of his tee shirt, but her effort was futile. "Hell, no. Don't you think, though, we should move out of sight somewhere?"

He grunted and released her hands. She rubbed the imprint of his hand on her wrists, wishing the mark would stay forever. She followed him to the inside of the shed where bags of grain lay stacked against the wall. Not scratchy like the hay, fifty pound bags of commercial grain were smooth against her skin as she plopped herself on top of the bags.

"No, switch." He stopped her motioning with his hand. "Ride me."

After last night, she shouldn't have been surprised nor bashful, but here in the middle of the day without any forgiving shadows of night, Evangeline hesitated, and her body grew cold. At least with him covering her, she hadn't felt self-conscious.

"What's wrong?"

She scanned the shed and the rays of sun coming through the doorway. "I, uh, it's just so bright. I'm not so sure I want you...to..."

"To what?" He rubbed her hips as she stood wedged between his reclined body and the boulder.

"Ugh." She stared at the ceiling, hoping for some divine gift of speech. "See me. To see me. It's so damn light, you're gonna see everything I have, and I mean everything."

Her chill vanished as warm hands skimmed her arms. "I know. I can't wait to see everything you've got. It'll be better even than what I've imagined."

She sighed. "Yeah, I'm not so sure about that. You yourself couldn't refrain from commenting on my appetite."

"And I told you it was nice to see someone who wasn't worried where that pancake was going to end up."

"Well, I worry about it. I usually worry about it after the fact."

He laughed so hard Evangeline wondered if the roof would come down on them.

"Drop your drawers, beautiful woman, and ride this stallion."

CHAPTER ELEVEN

A nickering behind her forced Evangeline to turn her head from Rick's chest to the sound. There, in the doorway, stood Star blowing throw her muzzle.

"Did you watch the whole thing?" she asked the horse. "I've done more new sex things in two days than I have my entire life, and now I have an audience."

"You deserve a little fun." Rick raked his fingers through her hair, making her scalp tingle and core take notice. As much as she appreciated and loved her awakening, a heavy dose of sadness draped over her heart.

"It took my entire adult life to experience something wonderful and special, but Ian never will, and I have a lot of regret about that. What if we'd faced up to reality sooner? He'd still be alive."

The rhythmic circles Rick's fingers traced over her back had at first lulled her into blissful existence, but thoughts of Ian crumpled her peace. Would she ever stop feeling guilty?

"Evie, I believe there are times and places for everything. Times and places we set, and times and places set in the stars. What do you think Ian would want for you?"

"He was the most unselfish person I've ever known. He'd be saying I was stupid for passing up an opportunity." As soon as the words left her mouth, an overwhelming sense of freedom passed through her body.

Rick wrapped her in his arms, and she could have sworn she heard a whisper of "Welcome Home" in the afternoon breeze.

"Did you hear that?"

"Your massive heartbeat? Yes, I can hear that miles away."

"No, I thought I heard...never mind." She rested her head against his chest again and counted the spaces between his heart beats. Almost two seconds.

"Sometimes, you end up in a place because you're supposed to be there. Evangeline Cortés, you're right where you belong. I know it, and there's some other things you have to know."

"Other things? Like what?" A tenseness rippled through his muscles, and Evangeline froze.

"Like, I've waited a long time for you to come into my life, and I don't want to do anything to make you not want to be in my life." The late afternoon sun shining directly on the shed had caused the temperature inside to rise. Both of their bodies were wet with sweat, and Evangeline's hands slipped when she tried to push up.

"Let's try that again." She managed to get enough grip to push herself upright. "Well, unless you're going to tell me to go on a diet, then we don't have a problem."

She gathered her clothes and began to dress. "Star, are you going to watch me get dressed, too? This feels weird."

Rick retrieved his own shirt and jeans from the floor. "Mares watch out for each other."

"I'm not a horse."

"I suppose not."

She thought she detected a hint of disappointment in his voice. "I'm going to go take a shower. Care to join me?"

A raised eyebrow gave her an answer.

"I know. No one in the guests' cabins." She moved

to his side and stood on tiptoe. Her lips brushed his ear. "I won't tell anyone."

"And yet, they'll all know." He kissed her forehead. "I'll meet you at dinner."

"It's hot dog and baked beans night," she said with childlike glee.

"Beans and wienies. That's what gets you excited?"

"Doesn't it everyone?"

CHAPTER TWELVE

Maverick and Keller sat chewing on straws from the bales of hay they sat perched on. This stack was in the barn, and with the horses fed and other cowboys washing up before dinner, they were alone. He and Keller didn't get a lot of time alone. There was always so much do.

"I think we're at a place where I need to say something." Maverick picked another straw from the bale and began to chew the end.

"When?" Keller stretched his long legs across the stack.

"Not sure. Definitely not tonight. I've got to clear my head, figure out what I want to say...and do. I've got to go to Storm Canyon tonight. I can't keep putting it off."

"You stayin' the night?"

"I think so. Don't worry. I'll be back before sunup to help." He'd lost some of the intoxication from his time spent with Evangeline. Now, the seriousness of what he had to do weighed on him like stones.

"Makes for a long night."

"I don't sleep much. You know that."

Keller yawned and stretched. "You know sleep is one thing I've really begun to appreciate in this life. It's highly underrated."

Maverick spit the chewed straw from his mouth and stood. "And unnecessary."

"Depends on what side of the canyon you're on. I think you could get used to havin' Miss Cortés snuggled up to you all night."

"Then we wouldn't be sleepin', for sure." He stuffed his cowboy hat on and turned to leave the barn. "See ya in the mornin'."

Keller raised his head in acknowledgement.

Evangeline wasn't sure if she should wait for Rick or grab her food now and get a table. Since the weather was warming, more guests had been arriving at the ranch, and the tables filled early. Her growling stomach made the decision, and she moved through the food line, avoiding the knowing smiles of Rose, Lara, and Dylan as they dished out the hotdogs, baked beans, and macaroni and cheese.

She found a partially empty table and sat one body space from the end to allow room for Rick. When he arrived, he filled a bowl with salad and joined her.

"That's it. That's all you're eating?" Evangeline said, feeling the dribble of bean sauce running down her chin. She wiped and set her napkin beside her plate.

"Not real hungry tonight."

"Something happen between two hours ago and now?" A feeling of dread rolled in her stomach, and the food no longer held its appeal.

His hand skirted up her spine before resting on the back of her neck. The public gesture of affection surprised her. Now, she was confused.

"Nothing but good happened. I've just got some things I've got to do tonight, so I can't spend any time with you." He winked. "And that disappoints me."

"It's campfire night. I haven't heard any good Buck stories lately, but I'll be alone in my cabin later, should someone decide to break a rule."

"You want to go on an overnight trip tomorrow"

Rick pushed away his bowl after only a few bites of lettuce.

"Overnight? Where? In Spearfish, Deadwood?"

"Outside."

"In a tent?"

"Under the stars."

RICK SAT atop a large bay gelding and extended his hand for Evangeline to take.

"Why are we only taking one horse?" She accepted his offer and allowed his strength to pull her up on the horse in back of him. She had no saddle, no stirrups, and her ass sat on top of a bedroll tied behind the saddle, while her legs dangled over the saddlebags, and the only way to keep from sliding off the horse's rump was to wrap her arms around Rick's waist. Maybe not such a bad thing.

"Makes it harder for you to get away when I take you to an isolated area of the canyon." He nudged the horse forward. "Or maybe, I like the feel of your arms squeezing me."

She rested her chin on his shoulder, taking in the fresh scent of a clean-shaven face. The sun was warm on her face. Sounds of the rushing stream, blowing breeze, birds, and bugs encompassed her. She couldn't remember a time when she'd felt happier, and deciding on a time to leave was getting harder and harder.

They rode for a couple hours through meadows, copses of trees, and up and down hills, until he pulled the horse to a stop in a dense group of old growth trees. She'd never seen this part of the canyon, but she thought it was somewhere near where she and Rick had ridden the day she'd thought she'd heard other horses.

"We stopping here?" They were losing daylight fast, and Evangeline knew that night in the woods was blacker than pitch.

"Yep, hop down." Rick held her hand as she kept one arm anchored around his waist before dropping to the ground. He swung from the saddle and secured the horse's reins on a nearby bush.

"Please tell me you're going to make a fire...? I can't see shit once it gets dark."

"Really? I like the dark, but I'll start a fire. There might even be a marshmallow or two in the saddlebag."

Within a few minutes, they'd both gathered enough twigs, dried leaves, and wood for a fire. Evangeline unpacked the items Rick had in the saddlebags—water, granola, and marshmallows. She left the bedroll, assuming they wouldn't need it until later, or sooner, once the food ran out and they couldn't keep their hands off each other. Her discovery of how great sex could be was like getting a new Christmas toy. She could play with it for hours, day after day until she somehow broke it. She didn't believe she could break anything of Rick's, but she wondered if a broken heart lingered in the future.

The snapping and popping of a newly built fire broke her musings. She gathered the items and turned toward the fire. Darkness had descended, blanketing the entire area in a mantle of obscurity, except for the golden flames dancing in the night. She caught her breath at the sight of Rick illuminated by the glow. He'd removed his hat, and his hair and the night melded into one, but the rest of him, blurred by the reflection of the flames, seemed to loom larger than he was. He looked untamed and liberated from the requirements of life. Evangeline put her hand on her chest to see if her heart still beat. Damn, if he wasn't the most beautiful man she'd ever seen.

She commanded her legs to move, but they balked. For the first time, she noticed the silence. Only the crackling of the fire cut through the air. The night sounds had quieted as if holding their breath. The hairs on the back of her neck stood, and her head tingled. She glanced at her arm, wondering if she was really feeling blood flow through her veins.

Making her way back to the fire, she sat the provisions on the ground and began to lower herself to the ground beside him.

"No." His fingered encircle her forearm. "Here." He spread his legs, indicating that she sit in front of him. She complied and eased herself against his chest as he began to curl her hair around his fingers.

"You seem very hesitant all of sudden. What's wrong?" he asked.

"I don't know. Something is happening, but I don't know what. It's scaring me a little."

Kissing her cheek, Rick placed his arms across the top of her chest. "I won't let anything happen. You're safe here. Tell me some more about you."

"We've already had this conversation." Even with his lips nuzzling her ear, Evangeline found relaxing difficult.

"I know, but tell me about your home, Santa Barbara. The area, what's it like?"

Why was he asking? Was he wanting her to re-familiarize herself with her home because he didn't want her stay here? Or was he thinking about visiting her? Or was he stalling for something else?

"Well, um…" She sighed. "They call Santa Barbara the American Riviera. It's a beautiful coastal city. Perfect weather. Flowers everywhere. Rich people everywhere. It's a great place, but I've considered moving across the mountain to Santa Ynez."

"Why's that?"

"Santa Ynez has this real eclectic mix of horses, cattle, wine country, regular folk and money, all in one little valley. Life is a lot slower there. You can eat breakfast in a dive and dinner at a winery. People are nice there." She leaned forward and turned to him. "Why are you asking me? Do you want me to leave?"

He jerked her back against him. "No, I don't want you to go. I was trying to get a feel for how you feel about your home. It's a very different life from here."

A sense of relief began to weave through her. "Different doesn't mean bad."

"No, but you have to drive a long way to see the beach or five-star restaurants, and the truth is, that's something I could never do. I can't leave here. I've… there's just too much I'm responsible for."

"Your family and business." She settled again, luxuriating in how perfect her body fit against his.

"That, and other things. I don't see myself being able to function anywhere else, but you…you have another life."

The flames were starting to die down, and Rick handed her another piece of wood to stack on the fire. Right now, sitting here in his embrace, she didn't want to be anywhere else. She loved the simplicity of the ranch. Not that it wasn't hard work. Everyone on the ranch put in well more than eight hours every day, but they seemed happy to do it. Before she'd come here, she'd put in more than eight hours, but a chunk of that time had been spent commuting to various job sites. The days she'd worked from home hadn't been as plentiful as she would've liked. Since Ian died, and even before, life had become very mundane. Even the beauty of coastal life wasn't enough.

She fiddled with the rough skin on his knuckles. His hands weren't soft. They were rough and calloused but always gentle. "I love my mom and my sister. I miss them. I haven't been very good company in the last few years. I mostly hear that I need to move on with life. I'm sure they didn't think that me moving on would land me here."

"I'd like nothing more than seeing where we go, but before any of that can happen, you need to know some things."

She felt his grip tighten.

"I'm not everything you think I am."

"So, you're more than a hot, sexy cowboy with a

golden heart?" His tense hold didn't ease any with her joke, and her earlier trepidation returned.

"You know the nights you saw the white horse?"

"Uh-huh?" *What does this have to do with anything?*

"It wasn't a ghost horse."

"I know that. I'm not sure I believe in that kind of stuff—you know, all the paranormal stuff people talk about. I think it's all hype for money."

"Okay…"

"I'm more of a show me the money kind of girl." Rick's chest began to rise and fall in a fashion she'd never noticed before. Fast and shallow. She'd always thought his slow hearts and breaths were fascinating.

"Show you the money," he mumbled and sighed. "Evie. The horse is real because it's me."

Had she heard him correctly, or was the crackling of the fire way too loud?

"Evie?"

"Did you say you were a horse?" She whipped her body around to face him. He couldn't possibly had said what she'd heard.

"Yes."

"But you aren't, now?"

"I can switch back and forth."

She wished he'd smile. Tell her he was joking, but the longer she stared, the more she was sure he believed what he said. Her heart was in her throat, and the black night began to close in on her like a hungry wolf.

She scrambled to her feet and stumbled away from the fire and him, *or it*. She wasn't sure what she was hearing He began to rise. "No," she pointed. "Stay the fuck away. You're insane. You give me the best days and sex I've had in my life, and now you're telling me I've been fucking a horse! You're insane."

Suddenly, she was choking. She clawed at an invisible rope, tightening around her neck. All her fingers touched was skin, but sure as the world she was choking, and her heart was breaking.

"Please, don't move, and let me show you. Don't run, please, you'll get lost." He rose slowly—his shadow from the fire casting over her like a monster.

Glancing over their surroundings, she knew he was right. She couldn't see a thing, and getting lost in the forest wasn't how she wanted things to end. Besides, her body was so frozen right now; she doubted she could move anyway.

They stared at each other across the fire. He stepped back from the flames, but his body never disappeared from her sight. Evangeline blinked several times attempting to focus as Rick's outline became blurry, and then disappeared altogether. As the blurriness cleared, across the fire, once again stood something. Not Rick. Not the man who'd awakened her body and soul. Her mind flashed to the night she'd drank the bad whiskey and to the night she'd gone to visit Star in the corral—the night she'd seen the magnificent silver stallion glowing in the night.

A wavy black mane fell long along his neck, and his silver coat shimmered. She wasn't choking anymore, but her breaths were so rapid, she knew she'd pass out if she continued. Drugs. Maybe, somehow, he drugged her, and she was having hallucinations. No. Why would he do that? He wouldn't. She was the one who was going insane. After everything that had happened—the almost divorce, Ian's murder, her inability to cope, she'd finally snapped and lost her tenuous hold on her reality.

The horse stepped away from the fire and walked to her.

This is not real. This is not real.

When he was a few paces from her, he stopped and lowered his head. Shaking, Evangeline stretched her hand to him but too much space still divided them. She had to force herself to go to him. One. Two steps. Again, she stretched her hand to touch the velvety fuzz of the horse's muzzle. Its lips fumbled over her fingers, and she jerked her hand back. Her frantic breaths had stopped, but now, she feared she'd stopped breathing altogether. Extending his muzzle to her, the horse pawed the ground once. Evangeline allowed her fingers to rub along his jaw. A familiar scent called to her, and when she stared into one dark eye, she saw pleading and fear, and then a veil of black encompassed her.

CHAPTER THIRTEEN

E vangeline opened her eyes to find herself cradled in Rick's arms.

"You fainted," he said.

Nodding, she said, "I think I was hallucinating."

A sadness crossed his face. "No, you weren't hallucinating. I'm afraid I've hurt you, but you had to know."

Tears pooled, and then rolled down her cheeks. "I don't understand this. This can't be real."

"I know you don't understand. I didn't know how to tell you, but it's very real. It's my life, and I can't change it."

"Can you take me back to the ranch?"

"Right now?"

"Please, if you can see, will you take me back?"

He nodded as he wiped a tear from her cheek. "I can see. We'll go now."

Unsure if she would be able to hold on, Evangeline chose to ride in front of Rick in the saddle. His arms were still snug and warm around her, but she didn't find peace there as she had before. No, so many questions swirled in her head. Would she ever ask them? He'd betrayed her. She'd allowed herself to feel again, and he'd destroyed her.

EVANGELINE HAD HAD enough protein bar, chips, and water stashed in her cabin that she'd been able to hole up and lock the world out for two days. Since she'd returned in the early morning hours, she hadn't spoken to anyone. Her first instinct was to call her mom, but how does one call up their mother and say "Mom, my new boyfriend just told me he's a horse. How do you handle that?"

Whatever she'd expected from the overnight wasn't what she'd gotten. She'd been falling and falling hard for Rick, and one admission had destroyed everything. How could that even be? Stories of werewolves were stories, folk lore, nothing more. People didn't change into animals. How could he explain turning into a horse? Had he been get kicked in the head, and somehow the force transformed him.

And stallions fucked everything. They here the herd leader and got to poke every mare in the group. So, on those nights he'd been running around as a horse, had he been ramming his dick into every mare on the ranch? What had he been doing the night she'd seen him with Star?

Her life was too unbelievable to be real.

A knock on the door startled her from her mind's rants. She'd told housekeeping she didn't want any service. She'd tell them again she didn't want or need anything. The shower hadn't been used since they'd returned to the ranch.

She opened the door to find Rick on the other side. "Oh, now, you're going to break the rules. I'm not interested, or better yet, I can't deal with this right now."

"Well, I can't either. Let me in."

She shifted her shoulder enough Rick pushed through the doorway and didn't stop until he was braced against the small counter holding the coffeemaker and mini fridge. "I'm sorry. I didn't know what to do. I've never, never had any feelings for anyone like I have for you. Would you have wanted to continue this relationship and never known the truth?"

"I could have been okay not knowing. I'm pretty good at sticking my head in the sand. It's easier that way." Her legs were about to give way, so she yanked a chair from under the small table that sat near the window and collapsed. Two days hadn't made one bit of difference. Here stood the man she'd fallen for, and he wasn't man.

"Does your family know?" Had he kept the secret from Jim, Betty, Keller and everyone else?

Raking his hands through his hair, Rick's expression became even more exasperated than when he'd arrived. "When I told you we were family, even though I'm adopted, we're *family*."

Then they knew. A light went on inside her head. "Oh, dear God, all of you?"

He nodded. "Mom, Dad, Keller, Lara, Dylan, and Rose. Yes, all of us. The employees don't know, and we'd like to keep it that way."

Evangeline began to claw at her forearms. This couldn't be real. She had to be dreaming. God dammit, let her wake up from this.

"I wish you'd stop looking at me like I was a monster in your nightmare." He approached the table and pulled out the other chair. He sank his large frame on the wooden chair.

Evangeline, who had been leaning on her elbows, sat straight and moved her hands to her lap.

He wouldn't look up into her face and stared at the table. "I'm not going to touch you. I wouldn't dream of it, now. You know, for Keller and everybody else, it doesn't bother them. They traverse both worlds like it's nothing. But me, I've always felt like some kind of freak. That's why I shy away from most people, but with you, I couldn't help myself. I couldn't stay away, but I never felt more like a freak than I did when I saw the look on your face that night. It broke me."

When he raised his head, moisture brimmed in his eyes. "I did not, do not, want to hurt you. I hope you at least believe that." He shoved back the chair and stood. "I won't bother you anymore."

As he went through the door and closed it, the sound rattled through the wall like an earthquake crumbling her heart as easy as a sandcastle.

Her fingers gripped her hair as she rested her head on her hands. She'd killed Ian, and now, her hysterics had destroyed the one man who'd made her feel alive. She was down to one protein bar but didn't care. Once she crawled into her bed, who knew when she'd ever crawl out again?

When she opened her eyes, the cabin was dark and only a sliver of a moon provided any light outside the window. Evangeline rolled over and switched on the lamp on the bedside table. She needed to do a lot of things—make a plane reservation, arrange for transportation, pack, find a place to live, find another job. The task was too daunting. Instead, she opened the drawer and found the old Silver Spear Ranch pamphlet from her Dad's things. She opened the pamphlet to draw out the unopened letter addressed to her. Maybe twenty years was enough, and it was time to face another truth.

Dear Baby Girl,

I wrote these letters weeks before I left and asked your Mom to give them to you and your sister. I know. I'm a coward. I should have been a man and told you I had to leave and not make Mom break the news to you.

I guess that's part of the problem. I was never a very good man, and the responsibilities that went with it, I couldn't handle. Not loving you, because you and Lily are the world to me, and leaving you is breaking my heart. But I have to. The only way my soul will survive is to go someplace where I'm not a freak...where I can be who I truly am.

I found such a place in South Dakota, and for years, I tried going once a year to relieve my pain, but every time, leaving became harder and harder because this is the only place that is truly home for me.

Missing you, Lily, and your mom will be the hardest part of my journey because I know once I make the deci-

sion, I'll never be able to make myself come back to you. That alone is shattering my heart.

I know you will become a strong, talented woman, and my biggest hope is one day you will forgive me because I can never forgive myself.

I love you with all my heart,

Dad

Oh my God. Her dad. He was one of them. Evangeline snatched her phone from the table. As tears ran down her cheek, she pressed her Mom's number.

"Hi Eve. How are…"

"Mom, did you know?"

"Know about what, Baby?"

"About Dad."

An eternal silence seemed to fall between them, giving her the answer.

"Yes, Baby, I knew."

"And you? Me? Are we like that?"

"No, Evangeline…"

She pressed End and threw her phone across the cabin. She didn't care if she broke the damn thing. Her whole life had been a lie.

Was not telling the truth protecting someone? What happened when they found out? This was what happened—unable to move from a bed and not knowing when, or if, she'd ever find a life with any peace.

Watching the shadows of the night turn gray with the coming dawn, Evangeline never once closed her eyes, and now, hints of morning pink were coloring the sky. Lying in bed would not get her any answers—only more questions. She peeled off her clothes and turned on the shower for the first time in three days.

Streams of hot water eased some of the tension in her shoulders and the stiffness from lying for hours in bed. She wasn't a child. She was thirty-five years old, and she needed to stop acting like it. She'd get her answers and move on. Whether it be California or somewhere else in the world, she would move on with her life.

She found Rick at the corral brushing Star. The two had a connection deeper than man and horse. She saw it now. Star relaxed under Rick's watch. She didn't seem afraid anymore. A look of surprise registered on his face when he saw her coming up the path.

"Can you explain some things to me?" she asked, opening the gate to the corral.

Star nickered a greeting.

"Sure, as much as I can." He continued to run the brush down Star's legs.

Evangeline picked another brush from the bucket

at his feet and began to brush the mare on the opposite side of Rick. "How did all this begin?"

"You want a history of us?"

"Yes."

"Okay. It will explain some things." He stopped brushing the horse's leg and moved to run the bristles across her neck. "Hernán de Cortés traveled…"

"Cortés?" Evangeline raised an eyebrow.

"Yes, Cortés," he said with a nod. "He and his men traveled from Spain first to Hispaniola, and then on to Cuba. From there in 1519, they landed in Mexico, and if you know much about that history, it was a bloody one with his army massacring thousands and, basically, after a while conquered and pretty much destroyed the Aztec Empire. However, before that happened, there was a battle in Otumba where the army lost over eight hundred men. Many horses were wounded, as well. The wounded horses were left on their own. Many of them died, but after they wandered for days, some stumbled onto a spring hidden from the view by most. When they drank from the spring, their wounds were healed."

Rick moved to Star's tail still filled with brambles. He meticulously began to pick hair from the bramble. "Anyway, the small herd began roaming the countryside, and when they happened upon more soldiers near a village, the horses remained hidden in the trees, not wanting to suffer any more in battle. If they could find a way to travel without being detected, then they would be safe. The legend says that the horses were transformed into humans, and they walked right toward the soldiers like they were villagers. One of the soldiers spoke and asked who they were and where they were going. Words came from one of the horse people's mouth. One called himself Cortés and said they were traveling north. The soldier thought he was somehow related to *the* Cortés himself and allowed them to pass."

Evangeline's hand rested on the brush but never moved a stroke. She was so mesmerized by Rick's story, she couldn't concentrate on anything else.

He continued. "They traveled north as Cortés had said, and every time they encountered humans, they found they could transform and assimilate. Eventually, Cortés settled the group and established a community in Mexico. They lived as both human and horse. Over the centuries, their numbers multiplied, and many emigrated to the States. And that's where we are today…assimilated, and few know of our existence."

She swallowed. "I'm a Cortés."

"Yes, you are related. Your father has direct lineage to the original Cortés."

"But why am I not…?"

Star sidestepped when Rick pulled one too many hairs from a tangled tale. "Because your mother is not one of us. Only two with Cambios blood can produce another. However, a half a Cambios and a full Cambios can produce another."

"Cambios?"

"Everyone who can change has Cambios in their heritage name."

Rubbing her forehead, Evangeline said. "Damn, Cambios-Plata. Silver Changes. Right in front of me."

"You couldn't have figured that out. It's, um, too weird."

This time she managed a few strokes across Star's back. "Is my father still alive, and is he here?"

Rick met her gaze. "He's alive. He reverted."

Thoughts were like needles in her brain. Her head hurt from all Rick had told her. "I can hardly process any of this. He's like fifty-five years old. Horses don't live that long. How could he still be alive?"

"It's a little complicated, but basically, as we age, we have to decide how we want to live, because the older we get, the harder it becomes to change back and forth. At a certain point, you can no longer change. If you decide to remain human, you will age as a human does. If you remain as a horse, you age as a horse in equivalent years. A horse who is thirty is the equal of a human who is about eighty-five. So, by reverting at age thirty-five, your father was roughly ten to twelve as a horse."

"So, he would be very old, right now."

"Extremely."

What would her dad look like as a horse? Would he even know who she was? "Can I see him? Where is he? Do you know him?"

He dropped Star's tale and moved next to Evangeline. He looked and smelled the same, but he carried a sadness that showed in his stature. "I know him. He's in Storm Canyon. The canyon is a refuge. Kind of a magical place really. Only a few places like it exist in this part of the country. It's a special place. Everyone there is protected from the extreme weather, and there's always plenty of food. It's my job to make sure it stays hidden."

"Will you take me there?"

He blew a breath through his lips. "I could take you there, but as far as meeting your father, I'd have to ask him first. I can't break his trust by not asking."

"Break his trust? He's my father. He left me, and I'd like to see him." As soon as she said the words, the pain of his leaving thrust a knife in her heart. How many years had she wondered if she'd been the reason he'd left? Even if she'd read the letter back then, she wouldn't have understood its significance. Now she knew, and her mind was reeling from the overload of information.

"I will ask him, but I can only go at night."

Star had grown impatient standing so still and walked away, leaving the two of them facing each other with no horse between them.

Evangeline stuffed her hands in her back pockets and rocked on her heels. "When we rode, and I thought I heard horses. Were we near Storm Canyon?"

"Sorta. Sound travels out here, but yeah, kind of close. We were right outside the entrance the night I told you. I wanted to show you, but things got out of hand." His gaze burned through her, and the attraction was still there, but she was afraid of what she still didn't know about Rick.

He turned toward the gate. "I've got to feed horses. I'll let you know."

The aloof cowboy she'd met when she'd arrived was back.

THE DINING AREA buzzed with the conversations of a room full of strangers. Evangeline accepted her food without ever making eye contact with Lara, Rose, or

Dylan. Rude, she knew, but with the information she had, everything was different.

She managed only two bites before Lara plopped herself across the table from her. "Look, I know things are a little weird, right now. It's really not that weird."

"For you, maybe." The normally, delicious mac 'n cheese felt like paste in her mouth. "No, Lara, it's weird. It's fucked up my whole world, so I'm sorry if I can't find the bright spot."

"Look at me." Lara's voice was no longer like her jovial self.

Evangeline raised her head, and what she saw was a woman with fire blazing from her eyes, anger piercing through.

"The world doesn't revolve around just you. Yeah, we're different. We have to adjust. We have to blend in, but we also have to hide. If people found out, we'd be the biggest circus side show of the millennium. Given all of this, we're still creatures who have feelings and need to love as much as we need to be loved. Our world is small, and for Maverick to allow you in and open himself up to be vulnerable, only to have you do exactly what you did and treat him like a fuckin' Cyclops, well, I guarantee he's done. Done, because he can't endure that pain again, and done, because you're the only one he's ever, ever said he loved. Thank you for stomping all over him."

Love? He'd never told her he loved her? She'd never told him either. She wasn't even sure what she was feeling was love. They'd only known each other a short time.

"Why would he agree to take me to Storm Canyon if I'm such a horrible person?"

Lara blew out a breath, and her shoulders drooped. "You're not a horrible person; you're in a bad place, right now. I can partially understand." Her fingers brushed across Evangeline's hand. "He understands, too, because he does love you, but he won't say it now."

After she left, the feel of Lara's fingers still lingered. How often had Rick's touch embedded itself into her soul? Even the nights she'd lain wide awake and alone, the memory of his touch gave her chills.

Her appetite gone, Evangeline left the dining hall and lingered on the porch. The path to the right went to the cabins and corral housing Star. The path to the left led to the barn. From her vantage point, she could see the barn and horses milling around in the corral, nibbling at the flakes of hay and grain in the trough.

Sunset wouldn't be for another hour, but hints of

the arriving dusk were all around. A quiet calm had spread over the ranch. Chipmunks were scurrying for their last bites of the day, and frogs along the creek were announcing the impending evening. She'd come to appreciate the sincerity of a fly-over state. South Dakota held a magic all its own, one she wouldn't have discovered if not for a rumpled brochure. The people were genuine, and the landscape still possessed a wildness she'd thought only remained in history books.

She saw Rick leaving the barn and walking toward the boulders where he'd opened her eyes to a new desire. Descending the wooden steps to the gravel path, she hurried after him, careful not to get so close he'd know she was there. When she passed the boulders, she caught a glimpse of him disappearing into the woods on the trail. Seconds later, she heard the hammering of hooves on dirt, fading through the trees.

Did he change every night? Was the freedom of running furious and unencumbered so intoxicating he couldn't live without it? Did they all do it together as a family? So many questions burned in her brain.

She passed the cowboy named Polk as she trudged up the path.

"Hey, you goin' on the sunrise ride tomorrow?"

he called to her. "There's only four signed up. Plenty of room."

"Thanks, Polk, but I think I'd like to sleep in a little tomorrow."

"Yes, ma'am. Goodnight." He tipped his hat and went on his way to the bunkhouse.

She smelled the aroma of the nightly campfire but wasn't in the mood to be social or hear any tall tales. However, sitting in her cabin held no appeal either. She decided to go visit Star. The horse had watched her have sex. Evangeline believed she could tell her anything now. Passing the ranch house again, she noticed a woman sitting in one of the porch rockers. Damn, it was Betty. She couldn't mistake the striking woman. She had a mass of dark waves without one strand of gray. Tall and solid, Betty Silver was an alpha mare, for sure.

Evangeline had never seen Betty sitting on the porch rockers since she'd been here.

"Evangeline." She patted the chair next to her. "Come sit for a bit. Such a beautiful evening. We should enjoy it."

Her stomach dropped to her knees. Whatever would she say to the woman? She opened her mouth to decline, but words failed her, so she shuffled to the waiting chair. "Hi, Mrs. Silver. Haven't seen you out here on the porch much."

"Every now and then, I wander down the hill to watch the evening visit us. Dusk is my favorite time of day. Time to reflect on the day and contemplate tomorrow." She rocked with the slow rhythm of a woman who had life all figured out and no need to worry.

Evangeline sat still. Any rocking she'd do would be frantic and warp the wood. "One of the things I love here is the peacefulness."

"Not been all that peaceful though, lately, has it?"

Was there anyone who didn't know?

"We're a close family, Evangeline. Necessity dictates it."

And she was a mind reader, too.

"When Maverick told me, I didn't react very well." She bit her lip for having made the understatement of her lifetime.

Betty's hand reached out and covered her own. Her nails were perfect, but her hands were showing signs of arthritis and thinning skin. Still, her hand was warm and comforting. "I'm not so sure you reacted so much differently than any other standard would."

"Standard?"

"We call a person who can't change a 'Standard' because they have the same standard life as everyone else."

"But, I'm not completely a Standard though, am I?"

Betty patted her hand. "No, Sweetie, you're not. You're not a Cambios, but you have the potential for creating a Cambios. You are what we call a 'Creative.'"

"Never was a big fan of labels," Evangeline muttered.

"We are who we are." Betty crossed her long legs, keeping the rocking rhythm with the tip of her shoeless toe. "Maverick couldn't help being attracted to you, because you carry some of our blood. He could sense it. But even the initial attraction wouldn't have gone anywhere if he hadn't really connected with you. His feelings are real. He's not just a stallion trying to carry on the line. In fact, I've had serious doubts Maverick would ever connect with anyone. He's always been different. His blood parents decided they wanted nothing to do the life and left him in the canyon not long after he'd been born. At least they came to us and told us. Jim went and found him, and I had just had Keller, so I suddenly I had two babies. So, he doesn't remember anything about them, and they've never returned." She pulled her hand away and rocked in silence.

"This is all a little much for me. I asked Maverick

to take me to see my dad, but I'm not sure if that will happen."

"Mav will do as your father wishes—not as you wish. His first responsibility is to those who live in Storm Canyon."

She nodded to herself. "Are you ever conflicted by who you are?" Her eyes widened at her own boldness. She hadn't meant to be rude. "I'm sorry. I-I shouldn't have said that. It's none of my business."

"It's okay. I wouldn't say I'm conflicted, but the older I get, the more I appreciate certain things available only in this life—soft beds, heating pads, a good whiskey." She raised a finger. "But, when my time is near, I'll revert and leave this world the way I came in. That's what I want."

Betty stopped rocking and stood. As if on cue, everything went silent. "Now, I think I'll go have some of that whiskey. Thank you for talking with me."

"Yes, ma'am. Thank you." Evangeline watched her glide her regal body across the porch and down the steps. *What a magnificent horse she must be.*

"Oh, Evangeline. I know you're conflicted, but I'll say this… If you were so convinced you want nothing to do with us, your ass would've been out of here days ago."

CHAPTER FOURTEEN

She was pushing eggs around her plate when Rick found her the next morning at the early bird breakfast. He didn't sit but leaned close to her ear to keep the cowboys from hearing. "Tonight. Can you ride bareback?"

"Yes."

"Meet me by the boulders when the sun goes down. We'll be gone most of the night, so get some rest today."

She had almost fourteen hours to kill. If she had a car, she could go into town. Sitting around the ranch all day would be torture. Hiking? No, hiking would make her tired. Reading? No, she'd read twelve books since arriving, and focusing on a new story would never happen now. Hot tub and wine? Hot tub and wine would make her sleepy… Since it was only six thirty in the morning, a nap would bring her up to lunch time and cut the waiting time almost in half.

While on paper, her plan seemed foolproof. In reality, the wine made her queasy, and the hot tub made her itchy. Once in bed, she never closed her eyes. Every nerve ending in her body exploded with electricity, shooting pain through her legs and head.

She'd been fifteen when her dad had left. What would she say to him, now? Would he look the same or would he seem old? She remembered her dad as a handsome man with dark eyes and hair. He'd seemed for very tall to her. She thought about calling her mom and asking more questions. She gathered her mom had not wanted her or Lily to know about their dad, so answering any questions now wouldn't change anything. She did wonder if Lily had ever read her letter. Lily was pretty much an open book, so she guessed she hadn't. Evangeline smiled. Her drama queen sister's wedding was in a few months. She had to leave to be part of the wedding. If she left, she wondered if she would return. Rick as a memory wasn't something she was ready to commit to as yet.

As the evening approached, she showered and lamented over what to wear. Since she'd be riding bareback, she couldn't wear a skirt. And why would she be riding bareback? She settled on jeans and the dark green tank with a denim jacket for the brisk ride.

With each step she took toward the meeting place, her stomach roiled with fear. Sweat pooled at the back of her neck and trickled down her spine. She should be excited, not paralyzed with dread. Two hours alone with Rick was a long time for trivial talk. While the sight of him excited her body, the memory of seeing him change would haunt her forever.

He was waiting by the boulders with his hands in his pockets, leaning against the rocks. Even his somber expression couldn't mar his handsome features.

"Where are the horses?" she asked.

He pointed to himself.

Panic rose in her. "No, I-I don't think that's the best idea."

He pushed from the boulder and closed the gap between them. "Trust me. It's the best way. We'll walk up in the woods a bit, and when we're out of sight, you'll wait. When I'm ready, jump on my back and hold on. Don't worry. I won't be able to talk to you then. So, you won't have to make conversation, but I can understand you if you're talking."

Evangeline's feet were frozen as Rick started up

the trail. Likely, the sound of only one pair of boots stopped him. He turned. "This is the only way. Your choice. I have no need to go back again tonight. This is for you."

Her dad hadn't been in her life for twenty years. Did it matter if she saw him again? Her mom and Lily had made a life without him because he couldn't be their father. He'd made the choice to leave them." She snorted and gritted her teeth. "Dammit, I'm going to tell you what I think about your choice."

She caught up to Rick where he waited. Within the trees, the light had faded, and she knew this was where he would change.

"Wait here. You'll know when I'm ready," he said.

He moved away from her and stopped close to a fallen tree. The blur of the other night returned as she watched but couldn't quite make out what was happening. When the fuzziness cleared, the creature standing in front of her resembled more of a normal horse than he had before. The sparkling sheen of his coat was gone, but he still sported a glorious color of silver with the black wavy mane covering most of his neck. His forelock draped across one side of his head. Muscles rippled from his chest to his withers and haunches, and a wild stare blazed from his coal-like eyes. He was indeed a maverick and magnificent.

He edged close to a fallen tree and tossed his head in the air. Evangeline swallowed. He was ready. As tall as he was, if he hadn't been standing beside the log, she would've had trouble mounting him. Grabbing two handfuls of mane close to his withers, she launched herself from the log and plopped onto his back.

She adjusted her grip on his mane and her ass on his back. Growing up, she'd ridden bareback all the time. Her friends and her would sneak into their neighbor's pasture at night and ride the horses. At first, they'd fallen off, but eventually, they'd learned methods to stay on. She loved the feel of nothing but horse between her legs but hadn't be able to ride bareback in years.

His muscles bunched as they climbed up the trail taking the same route they had a few nights ago. Evangeline found herself blushing when she remembered his words when they'd sex in the shed. "Ride the stallion."

So many things he'd said now made sense. "Mares watch out for each other," and "you have no idea," when she'd made a joke about him working with horses and being named Maverick. Even with the little clues, guessing his secret would've been impossible because animal shifters only lived in novels. She wondered what other animals on the ranch were disguised as people. Now, she would wonder if everyone she met was something else.

As they made their way deeper into the trees, the darkness made seeing difficult, and Evangeline's back, now wet from sweat, grew chilled. Her body flinched at every unidentifiable sound. She wasn't alone, but yet, she was.

"I talked to your mom last night. She told me about your parents. I'm sorry that happened to you. I felt abandoned, and I guess you do, too, maybe. If you never knew them, though, I suppose that might be better. Betty and Jim seem to be wonderful people. I don't really know them, but they must be. Everyone here seems really happy. I mean, if you had a crappy family, you probably wouldn't be too happy. My family wasn't crappy. I was mostly happy. Getting married like I did was a really dumb thing though. Neither one of us were really happy. We wasted a lot of years. I don't want to waste anything anymore."

Her body straightened with the deep breath she inhaled. "I'm rambling, aren't I? Okay, right, you can't answer me."

He bucked. Not a lot but enough she had to secure her grip again in his mane. "You want me to shut up?"

He snorted.

"What's that supposed to mean? Was that a 'no, keep talking' snort or a 'shut the fuck up snort'?"

He snorted again.

"That clears it up."

She quieted, but with being unable to see much of anything, the silence made her nervous. Quiet in the jungle, or forest, wasn't good. She scanned the sky full of clouds and wished for stars and a moon. Cloudy. How appropriate.

"Why is it called Storm Canyon? Oh, right. Another time. I'm about to ramble again. This whole thing is not only making me nervous but a little nauseous, too. You could say I've been off my feed lately. Not like me at all. I'm sorry I hurt you. I guess it doesn't really count, since you can't stare me in the face and tell me I was awful to you. But I really am sorry. However, what were you expecting? You have to admit I'm probably not the only person who would've reacted that way. I mean, come on. When I was a kid, I would go see werewolf movies because they scared the crap out me. You're not a werewolf. They're mean and ugly, and you're neither. You're very sweet and very hot. Someone who gets me wet just by walking into the room. I should shut up again, before—"

Like she'd been shocked, she retracted her hands from Rick's mane. His entire body was changing—not back into human, but his coat began to glow and sparkle like it had by the fire. He seemed not to notice the change and kept walking—walking into a wall of rock, she thought, at first, but which turned out to be a crack in the rocks, which widened enough for them to pass. They walked through the narrow passage, but light shone further down. Her hands began to shake, and she reburied her fingers into Rick's mane. They had to be close. Beads of perspiration popped on her forehead, and her deep, rapid breaths made her feel faint.

The brightness at the end turned out to be a moon casting light over a valley with a river dividing it. Evangeline estimated there were fifty horses on either side of the river. Some were eating. Some were galloping full speed across the grass, while others stood watching them approach.

Rick kept walking until they were well into the canyon. Evangeline slid from his back when he stopped. He let out a loud whinny, and several of the horses answered with their own. Although she didn't understand how it could happen, she was glad for the bright full moon in the sky over Storm Canyon.

Emerging from a small herd to her right came a

dull black horse. From his unsteady gait, she could tell the horse was old. Was this her father? The horse kept walking until he was only a few feet away. He stopped, and the two of them stared at each other.

"Daddy, I'm ready. You can change. I know what will happen."

The horse didn't move. Muscles ticked on his withers, making Evangeline believe he would change any second, but nothing. She turned to Maverick and was startled to find him standing there now as Rick. "Why won't he change? I want to talk with him."

"He can't, Evie."

"Why not?"

"Because he is near the end of his life, and if he changes now, he won't have the energy to revert. His wish is to leave this world as he came into it...as a horse."

She had no power to stop the tears racing down her cheeks. She hadn't seen her father in twenty years, and she still couldn't. The horse came to her, placing his lips on her cheek. His tongue licked her tears, which made her cry harder. She threw her arms around his neck and buried her face in the dark mane. The horse rested his muzzle on her back as she cried.

When she could cry no more, Evangeline finger-combed his mane. She then ran her hands across his sway back. Rick was right. Her father was at the end of his life. This night could be the only time she had to spend with him.

"Well, I have a lot to tell you." Evangeline began walking toward the river. She slowed her pace when she remembered her father's slow steps. "I only read your letter a few days ago. I was so angry when you left, I didn't want to hear anything you had to say. I tucked it away, and for some reason, when I decided to come to Silver Spear Ranch, I stuffed it into the suitcase. Maybe, it was some power guiding me. I don't know."

She sat on a rock near the bank. The sound of the river's current was musical and calming to her. Glancing around at the valley revealed in the rays of the moonlight, she understood the draw. It was protected by canyon walls, with an abundance of food, water, and plenty of places to run. This place would be heaven for anyone, not just horses.

Her father nuzzled her hand, and she began scratching the side of his face. "I didn't have a bad life. I just missed you. I thought we were a happy family. You were my best friend, Dad. I could tell you anything. No Daddy Daughter dances or camping trips. You didn't get to walk me down the aisle at my wedding. Although, well…that's another story."

She stopped scratching, and he moved his muzzle under her hand. "Okay. Okay, I'll keep on. You remember Ian? You should. He was always around. We played together constantly. Then we were a couple in high school." Her dad gave an irritated snort.

"I know. Well, it got worse. Still together in college because everyone said we were perfect together. One thing led to another, and we got married. It was a bad idea that stayed around for twelve years. We were getting divorced when someone murdered Ian. I've always felt it was my fault. I put him in that store."

He snorted again and nuzzled her hair. She remembered the times he used to ruffle her hair when she was little and upset. "Hey, you will beat this because you're my daughter," he'd tell her. Another tear began to form, but she wiped her eye before he could see.

"I found that brochure you had for Silver Spear. Something inside pushed me to come here. I've been here for a couple months. I guess I can sorta understand why you're here. I've never been happier…

well, until a few days ago. Then things got really complicated, again."

She noticed Rick had taken a seat against one of the trees, and several horses were gathered around him. "Daddy, I think I've fallen in love with Rick, but I don't know if I can live like this. This life. What if he's like you and decides he doesn't want to be a person anymore at all? What would I do? I'd be alone again, and what if we had a baby, and the baby could be a Cambios and both of them wanted to stay a horse. I'd lose both of them. I'd be standing on the sidelines, trying to answer questions I had no answer for. What happened to your husband? Where's your baby? If I told the truth, they'd put me in a psych ward."

Her dad began to nibble and pull on her sleeve. She shrugged, unsure of what he was doing. He circled her wrist with his mouth and pulled harder. She stood and said, "I don't know what you want?"

He then swung his head to his side again and again.

"You want me to get on your back?"

He swung again.

"Oh, Dad no. I can't. I'm not so sure your back can handle it. It's well known on the ranch that I like my groceries."

He stomped and pawed the ground.

Clasping her hands to her face, she pondered his request. She wanted to be close to him, maybe for the last time, but didn't want to hurt him. Even in his advanced years, he was still a big animal though. Rubbing her hands along his crest, Evangeline grabbed hold at the bottom like she had with Maverick and swung herself onto his back. A slight horse "oomph" escaped, but he began a slow walk along the river.

"You know, in my heart and in the back of my mind, I always knew I'd see you again. I think some people believed it was only wishes from a teenager who didn't have a bit of life experience. Funny thing is, now, I can't even go back and tell them 'told you so.' I suppose I can tell Mom. Now that I know, I can ask Mom all kinds of things like 'Did you know Dad was this way when you met?' If she did, she must have been crazy in love to accept the reality of who you really were."

With each stride, her dad's gait seemed to be easier and stronger. When she sought out Rick again near the horses, they were all gone. She shielded her eyes from the moonlight and spotted the group running at the north end of the canyon. Led by Maverick. His long powerful legs, stretched out to their fullest, seemed to skim the ground. They thundered down the bank and into the river, splashing and dispersing a wall of water like Moses and the Red Sea. Once they scaled the opposite bank, Maverick resumed his breakneck speed, leaving the others behind as he bucked and twisted his body across the meadow.

Her dad stopped and watched the procession of youth.

Evangeline rubbed his shoulder. "I bet you miss that." He whinnied and tossed his head.

Watching Maverick so jubilant and unburdened, she felt a pang of jealousy. *What must it be like to race to the end of your world and back?* This place was as magical as he'd said. She'd never fully grasp the instinctive need to roam, but she did have the instinct to need space and fresh air and nature. Maybe they weren't so different.

"I must be crazy in love with him," she mumbled to herself. Her dad tossed his head again. "Not a damn thing wrong with your hearing."

He resumed their walk, leaving the river behind and skirting the trees that lined the canyon. Sweet scents of honeysuckle and pine tickled her nose. This place was paradise for anyone, not just horses.

For a long time, Evangeline kept quiet. The rhythmic stride of her father lulled her into another world—a world where she imagined her life at the ranch with Rick and the rest of the family. In reality, they spent most of their time as people, and Rick's forays into his horse ego happened primarily at night. She preferred to sleep at night, and horses slept only a few hours in a twenty-four period, anyway.

She was so relaxed she almost tumbled from his back when he came to a stop. When Evangeline righted herself, she saw Maverick lingering by the entrance. *Time to go.*

The hours had seemed like minutes. She'd cried so much she thought all her tears were gone, but as soon as she slipped from her father's back, Evangeline's knees buckled, and she almost went to the ground. She moved in front of him and pressed her face to his forehead. He was there. The man she remembered hugged her back in the only way he could, by rubbing his forehead against hers. A bond she'd thought was lost was reborn with new power, strength, and healing. He couldn't speak, but he loved her. Evangeline was sure her father had loved her, but his pain had been so overwhelming, not even love could have kept him with her and the family. She'd once believed there were no limits to what love could overcome. This canyon was filled with the limits of love.

Maverick whinnied to her. She had to leave now.

"Um," her voice had grown hoarse, "I, uh, we have to go."

She sniffed and wiped her nose with her sleeve. "This has meant so much to me. It's breaking my heart to leave you, but I understand." Her jaw and mouth began to tremble. "I say that, but I'm not sure I really do. Even so, being with you tonight has been precious. I hope it was for you, too."

She kissed his nose. "I love you, Daddy."

He blew all over her shirt.

Through her tears, she gave a choking laugh. "Now, you know horse snot does not come out of a shirt." She gave him one last scratch under his chin and turned.

"Bye. I love you."

Because there was no log nearby, Maverick lowered himself enough she could mount. As soon as she grasped his mane, he straightened, and his coat turned the familiar sheen. Before they entered the passage way, Evangeline turned to see her dad one final time. He looked so regal, standing so straight and poised. He threw his head to the sky and called to her.

Unable to look again, she fell forward and rested the side of her head along Maverick's crest. In her mix of joy and grief, her body gave out, and Maverick's slow and steady trek to the ranch rocked her in and out of dosing.

When they stopped, she still slept. Only the quiet nickers from Maverick roused her. She jerked herself awake and hopped from his back. The drop in the dark was more than she'd anticipated, and she fell to her knees. By the time she stood and brushed the dirt from her jeans, Rick was back and standing beside her.

"Are you okay?" he asked.

"Yeah, just didn't stick the landing."

"Sun will be up in an hour. I suspect you'll sleep a lot today." He pointed to the wet spot on her shirt. "You know that usually doesn't come out very well."

She stretched the shirt for a better view. "The snot? Nope, it doesn't, but you know, I don't care. It's all I have of him."

"You have your memory."

"I do, and I wouldn't have that if you hadn't helped me. Thank you."

He gave her a curt nod and began to walk.

"Rick."

"Yep?" he answered as he stopped.

"Um, I." A sudden coughing fit and drainage forced her to clear her throat several times before she could speak. "Sorry. A lot of trail dust, I think."

"Probably." A sad smile crossed his lips.

"Would you…could we talk tomorrow?" She slid her hand to her throat in a nondescript manner to check her pulse. Surely her heart had stopped, waiting until he answered.

"If that's what you'd like."

"I would."

"When you wake up, come find me. I'll be with Star. I have to decide what to do with her."

CHAPTER FIFTEEN

Evangeline woke both exhausted and exhilarated—and not until after three in the afternoon. She hurried into the shower, anxious to see Rick and have their talk. The night spent with her dad, while sad at times, made her believe she could manage both worlds. Riding on his back, spilling her guts, had released her demons in so many ways. This morning, she felt lighter—her mind clearer—and, for once, she could say in all honesty, she was ready to determine her own happiness.

She wasn't even hungry either. After toweling off, she grabbed the first clean things in the drawer and didn't bother to see if they matched. Five minutes with the blow dryer seemed like an eternity and only managed to take her hair from wet to "oh, the hell with it." Flip flops over boots. Boots took too much time. A couple swipes of mascara, which she even questioned. Most of her time with Rick had been sans makeup. Quick spritz of body spray, and she had her hand on door ready to lay it all on the line.

"Mom!"

Julia Cortés stood poised to knock while holding a piece of luggage in her other hand. "Eve."

"What are you doing here?" Oh, God. This was not how she'd thought this day would start.

"After our phone call, if you'd call it that, I thought it would be a good idea to come and spend some time here and help you."

"Help me? I don't need any help, but I do have somewhere to go." Her heart raced, and a little anger began to form in her head. *She was silent for twenty years, and now, she wants to talk?*

"Are you going to let me in? Traveling here is a bitch. It'd been quicker on a stagecoach, I think."

With a sigh, Evangeline reached for her mom's suitcase and opened the door wide. Julia entered and made a sweeping scan of the cabin.

"Not much has changed at this ranch in twenty years."

"You've been here before?" The shock of her

mother's words was like someone swung a bat to her head. "When? Why?

Julia continued her examination. "Right after your father left. I came here to talk some sense into him and to keep him from abandoning our family. A lot good that did. His selfishness destroyed our lives."

Evangeline's joy from a few minutes ago lay crushed on the wooden floor—stomped over by a woman who hadn't even told her own daughter what had happened. "Still, I'm not so sure why you thought you had to come all the way here, when a phone call would have sufficed. Or better yet, not waiting twenty years to enlighten me concerning the truth."

"Evangeline, honey, at the time, I didn't think the truth was something you could handle." Julia sat her purse on the table and collapsed onto a chair. "Come sit down, so we can talk."

She followed her mom's order and joined her at the table. "Mom, I was a teenager, not a toddler."

"I didn't want you to be angry and confused."

Who was this person who looked like her mother? Evangeline leaned across the table, her face red with anger. "I was angry and confused. I had no explanation for why my dad left. Why didn't you tell me when I was twenty or twenty-five—or thirty? Hell, you could've told me before I even came here."

"I didn't really expect them to blab everything. I at least thought they'd have some discretion." Julia began digging through her purse, tossing items on the table. She snapped open a bottle of pain reliever and swallowed two without any water. "My head is pounding."

Hell, my head should be the one pounding.

"Nobody blabbed anything. I knew nothing until a few days ago, and that was only because Rick and I have been…"

"Don't you even say it." Her mom's eyes filled with fury. "You're not falling for one of these freaks, are you?"

"Mom, did you know about dad when you married him?" She'd never seen her mom so angry. Evangeline remembered when her dad left, her mom being very stoic about the whole thing, not even mentioning his name, or even acting like she was upset. It was like he'd never happened.

Julia began rubbing her forehead. "I knew. He told me, but he acted like he loved me so much, I didn't think it would be an issue, until it was. He wanted to move here, so he could go run around in that canyon. We had a life. You girls had a life. I wasn't about to uproot us to live out in the middle of nowhere. He just needed to try harder."

"But he gave you fifteen years of trying. Couldn't you have given him a few years of trying?"

Julia reached her hand across the table to caress the back of Evangeline's hand with her thumb. "Eve, I don't want you to go through the hurt I did. I want you to be happy."

"Mom, I spent twelve years in a marriage with someone I wasn't in love with. We weren't in love with each other. Look at all those years Ian and I wasted. I'm only now beginning to let go of some of the guilt I feel for him never having found happiness. I'm almost a middle-aged woman. I deserve to find my own life, my own happiness."

Evangeline's thumb squeezed the side of her mom's hand. "Even before Rick and I became involved, this place gave me peace. Made me feel whole again. Even if things don't work out for Rick and me, I won't be going back to California. I belong here."

"I'm afraid for you." Her mom's brows furrowed.

"I'm a big girl." She poked a finger in the waistband of her jeans. "And getting bigger since I've been here."

Evangeline had never seen her mom as a vulnerable person. She was strong and worked hard to take care of her and Lily. She'd been too wrapped up in her own self to notice if her mom had ever cried or needed someone to lean on. "Why didn't you ever remarry?"

A single tear trickled down her cheek. "I didn't believe I could ever love anyone else like I loved your father."

A huge lump lodged in her throat. Her own tears began to pool. "Mom, he's still here. He's not doing so well, but I could take you to him."

Julie began shaking her head. "No, no, I can't. I can't make my last memory of him be...that. I need to remember him as I knew him."

"I get it. It was hard, but it meant the world to me to know what happened."

"So, you're not going to come home?" Julia wiped another tear and tore through her bag again. She pulled a tissue from inside and blew her nose.

"I feel I am home. Watching Maverick running through the canyon was beautiful and mind blowing. I wasn't upset. I think I was a little jealous—to be that free. I can't imagine ever finding something that will give me that same feeling."

"So, I've wasted a lot of frequent flyer miles." She laughed and blew her nose again.

"You have. Although, you could answer me a question."

She sniffed. Her perfectly applied makeup had faltered, and she now sported raccoon eyes. "Ask away. I'm now going to be completely honest about everything."

"What was sex like with Dad?"

Her mom's face grew red. "Mind-blowing."

CHAPTER SIXTEEN

With her mom having already booked a return flight and now taking a shower, Evangeline hustled up the path to Star's corral. Her heart swelled knowing her mom had never lost her love for her dad. She understood her mom's fears for her. She wasn't without some anxiety and apprehension.

As she approached the corral, she saw Star nibbling at the dusty ground. The horse raised her head and pricked her ears, but there was no sign of Rick. He'd been and gone, probably feeling she wasn't interested enough to make the effort.

Unlatching the gate, Evangeline entered the corral and secured it again. "C'mere, Star. I may have missed my opportunity and lost my nerve. Let me unload on you."

Star jogged to her. What a different horse she was from the horse she'd met weeks ago. She was beginning to fill out, and her coat wasn't nearly as raggedy as when she'd arrived. Rick had done an amazing job with her.

"How's my sweet girl?" she asked, rubbing behind the horse's ear. Star responded by lowering her head for more scratching. "Was Rick here? I'm sure he was. How long did he wait for me? I have an explanation. My mom showed up. Can you believe my mom came all the way here to tell me stuff she should have told me decades ago?"

Star snorted.

"I know. She also tried to tell me falling for Rick is a bad idea. Too late. I said some bad things to him. I'm not trying to justify it, but I was so shocked. Maybe if I'd known about my dad, it would have been different. I suppose the potential for having more problems than most couples is there.

"You know something?" Evangeline stopped scratching and went to the shed. As soon as she entered, she smiled remembering how Rick had fucked her there, so thoroughly, she'd thought she was in another world. "We should try something."

She grabbed a saddle blanket and left the shed. "Let's see how you feel about this." With a slow and measured ease, she placed the blanket on Star's back. Star's skin rippled several times, but she didn't get excited. "Not so bad, is it? Let's walk."

Evangeline began parading around the corral with Star on her heels. "I wouldn't ask him to choose like my mom did, but I can tell you I do have some concerns about children." She scoffed. "Listen to me, I'm worried about my horsey children, and I don't even have any assurances about my future with the horsey man. On top of that, I'm getting a little close to the mom cutoff point. Children may not even be an issue."

She stopped, and Star stopped. Evangeline turned. When she waved her hand in the air, Star flinched. "Oh, sorry. I'm supposed to be finding my happiness. Damn, girl, can we just start with that?"

They circled the corral several times before Evangeline removed the blanket and fed Star a cup of grain. She was ignoring the fact Rick always fed her before he left for the day. Too bad. "A girl needs her groceries. You want a flake of hay, too?"

She left the corral to walk around to the back of the shed. Evangeline jumped when she saw Rick sitting on a bale of hay with a straw dangling from his mouth. Damn, he was hot. "Shit, you scared the crap out of me."

"What are doing?" he asked without removing the straw.

"I was looking for you."

"Star's had all the food she needs for the day."

The sudden wave of heat told her she was red from head to toe. "So, you heard me talking to her?"

"Most of it. Any questions you want to ask me as opposed to a horse?"

"Well, technically…"

The chewed straw dropped when he began laugh. "Come sit, and I'll answer your questions.

Being on his lap again was heaven. "This one has really been bothering me. Aren't you afraid of getting colic or something? I mean you took me to a steak place. That can't be good."

"That's what you want to know?"

"Well, that may be like number thirty six on a list of a thousand."

"Okay." He chuckled and blew out a breath.

Evangeline closed her eyes as he threaded his fingers through her hair.

"My body can digest in whatever form I'm in… for a time. If I ate like that every day, there would be a problem. I tend to eat a lot salad."

Another question was ready to roll out of her mouth when he grasped her hair and pulled her head to his face. His free hand brushed her cheek and thumb stroked her mouth.

"Evie. The most important thing you need to know is I love you. Now, I'm not a love conquers all type, but this where we start. I love you, but I cannot change who I am. I will not leave here. I will not let go of my responsibility to Storm Canyon. They depend on me to keep it secret. That's why they come…to keep their secret.

"I'll do everything I can to make you happy. You're important to me. I've never met anyone I wanted to be with more than you." He released her hair and planted a kiss on her forehead.

Damn, but she was beginning to feel tears well up, again. She was getting quite annoyed with her inability to control her emotions. "I love you, too. I am worried about you changing your mind and wanting to remain a horse, and I do worry about having a child who can change. I'd be afraid of losing my child."

"In answer to the first part, I won't make that decision. I do love my freedom and running and rolling in the grass, but like Mom, Dad, Keller, Dylan, Lara, and Rose, there are some perks of this world I don't want to give up either. As far as a child, I can't give you an answer, but I won't allow that decision until he or she is an adult in this world. You have to be able to completely understand both worlds to, not only straddle them, but survive. A child cannot make such a life altering decision."

A whole world of relief flew like a bird from her. "I can live with that. One other thing. You said you had to make a decision about Star. You've never had a saddle on her, so you can't make her a trail horse. Are you going to take her to the sanctuary?"

Losing Star would hurt. Star had become a friend. They'd needed each other.

"She can't be a trail horse. I couldn't trust her not to get spooked with guests. I'm not taking her to the sanctuary, either."

"What are you gonna do?" God, he couldn't sell her. She'd been through too much.

"I thought about giving her as a gift…to you."

"To me? Oh God, that would be…oh, my God, thank you." She flung her arms around his neck and slapped kisses all over his face. "I love you."

He'd talked about the sanctuary but had never told her where it was. "I'd like to visit the sanctuary, someday, if you don't mind."

He cocked his head. "You've already been there."

She twisted so fast in his lap, a loud grunt came from deep within Rick's throat.

"Storm Canyon? I would never have known that not all those horses were…Cambios."

"If I can't find another solution, I take them there. The weather never gets below freezing or above eighty degrees. Plenty of food, water, and company. It's the perfect place, and I can go check on them." He shifted Evangeline's body, flopping her legs across his lap and gathering her close.

"That's amazing. One thing. When we were close to the entrance, your coat got all glowy, kind of sparkly. Why?" A contented warmth filled her body. His lap was every bit as comforting as his back.

"It's a pass, of sorts. Only we can activate the portal. All of us have the genetic code for passing through it, but everyone who wants to go through has to go through a vetting process. Not all of us are, uh, looking out for the best interests of everyone."

"How do you vet a horse?"

"It's complicated to explain, and I have something else I'd rather do now." He placed his lips on hers. Evangeline welcomed him, opening her mouth and pushing her tongue against his. She leveraged his head hard against hers. She wanted everything he offered and more than she thought she could handle, but damned if she wouldn't die trying. She'd go through everything all over again to have this moment. He was different. He was otherworldly. He couldn't be explained. He was everything she needed.

She pulled back her head and gave him a hard stare. "One last thing. As a general rule, one stallion has a whole herd of mares…"

He cupped her chin, forcing her to meet his gaze. "There's only one mare."

"Good to know, because I've helped geld a few stallions before."

CHAPTER SEVENTEEN

K eller tossed Julia's bag into the back of the pickup as Evangeline gave her mom a hug.

"I promise I'll be back for Lily's wedding," Evangeline said, "but I'm not staying long."

Julia's hug was powerful, and Evangeline thought she'd snap her in two.

"You know, honey, I only want you to be happy."

From the corner of her eye, she caught Rick and Keller talking. He seemed none the worse for wear after their all-night, wickedly primeval love-making session. Every step she took made her want to scream, but her throat was too sore. Him going off at night, on occasion, might not be such a bad thing. She didn't have the stamina he did but wasn't about to complain.

"Mom, I am happy. I've never had a time in my

life where I was excited about every day. I realize I'll be challenged, but I guarantee I'll never be bored."

"That's what I needed to hear. Love you, Baby."

"Love you, too."

Her mom got in the truck, and Rick went to the window. Evangeline cringed when her mom grabbed the front of his shirt and yanked. She couldn't hear what her mom was saying. All she saw was Rick nodding.

She released his shirt, and Evangeline heard a "Yes, ma'am."

The truck lurched forward, and they were on their way. When they had disappeared down the lane, Rick came to her side and wrapped his arm around her waist. "You're sure of this, right?"

"Never more sure, why?"

"Because you and your mom toss around the word *gelding* way too much."

"So, tell me, how did you get out of driving my mom to the airport? You guys flip a coin?"

"Negotiated. I told him if he drove her to the airport, I'd take the Saturday midday ride."

Evangeline side-eyed him. "I think you got off easy."

"I did, because I figured you'd go with me. See, it's a bachelorette party…"

"Oh, Hell no. No, no, no. The level of stupid of

women at a bachelorette party is beyond measure. And they will be throwin' their best stuff at you. It just might be worth going just to watch you squirm."

"You are an evil woman." He winked, and her legs turned to butter. "Want to show me how evil you can be?"

She thought of how every muscle in her body screamed for a hot tub and a glass of wine. With a sigh, she said. "No pain. No gain. Let's go cowboy."

The End

ABOUT THE AUTHOR

I've spent most of my professional life as a sports writer for various publications. When not working, my husband and I make the most of our lives with family, friends, travel, sports, and music.

Born and raised in Indiana, I attended Indiana University and graduated with a B.A. in Journalism. My husband and I have lived in six states but have returned home to central Indiana. We've had a multitude of foreign exchange students and currently live with three parrots, Kiaga, Buddy, and Simon and two dogs, Lucy and Raven.

Thanks for reading. I'd love your feedback and reviews.

Visit me at my web site at www.annahague.com
Facebook: www.facebook.com/annahagueauthor
Twitter: @AnnaHagueAuthor
Instagram: AnnaHagueAuthor